Fatal Flip

A Home Renovator Mystery

by

M. E. Bakos

ISBN: 979-8-9850770-6-3

Printed in United States of America

For my husband, Joe Sebesta,
and Chipper

CHAPTER 1

I stood on a rung of the stepladder, looking into a black hole of the attic access in the closet of the house I was rehabbing.

"Dang it! Dang. Dang," I said, sputtering, my heart racing.

"What?" My best friend, Myra asked, puzzled, as she waited for me. Myra Alexandria Payten was nervous about heights, even six-foot stepladders. She wasn't a fan of peering into remote areas of homes under renovation and waited while I inspected the attic.

"It's a body," I said, gasping. "A body that hasn't moved for a while." My legs quivered, and my knees buckled. Gingerly, I stepped down the ladder to face a flabbergasted Myra.

"You have got to be kidding!" she said, each word short and clipped, staring at me openmouthed. Myra always used proper English, even under stressful conditions.

"I kid you not." Dread settled in the pit of my stomach. "I hate it when that happens." When faced with panic-inducing situations, I can be understated, stoic.

"We must call the police immediately!" Myra gasped; her hazel eyes wide.

"Yep," I replied resolutely. "We must."

I felt badly about the body we'd just found in the attic. The poor soul could have been there a while, but any smell was held at bay in the cool Minnesota spring. The heat was off in the house, and the body was well-preserved—for a dead person.

The dread in the pit of my stomach was terror about my present finances. This was my job now; I was a house renovator. Just a step up from a slumlord.

My name is Katelyn Baxter. I am thirty-five years old. I admit to twenty-eight, because twenty-nine is a cliché. I've been married twice. Once divorced, from my high school beau, Eddy. Now widowed, from the love of my life, Jake.

My business card says I am a Home Renovation Specialist. I love anything related to home repair and renovation. So much so, when I was dismissed from my position at a mega medical organization, I decided to become a house flipper.

A year earlier, my boss, Michael Preston Ness, chief communications officer, had summoned me to his office. Someone in marketing was going to take a hit for the team, a demotion to 'records coordinator.' I was the one selected to take the hit.

"No!"

He glared at me from across his desk, his face turning an impressive blotchy red, a blue vein bulging in his forehead.

"What!"

"Hell, no!" My face felt hot, and was likely as red as his.

By the end of the day, Janice from Human Resources and Michael Preston Ness marched to my cubicle, took my key and employee pass card. In a final humiliation, I was told not to talk to anyone at the hospital. I presumed, that meant friends, as well.

That evening, while calling everyone I knew, I finished a fresh bottle of chardonnay. My hangover lasted a day. The rest of the week, I lay on the sofa, watched cartoons, and ate Doritos.

I will refrain from naming this goliath company in the event they could sue the heck out of my penniless soul, and I am somewhat paranoid.

This is how I came to renovate the house on Bluebird Street in Crocus Heights, Minnesota. It was in a "transitional" neighborhood where streets were named for birds—Robin, Hawk, Jay, etc. The neighborhood had seen some decline, but was becoming fashionable again, with close proximity to amenities, public transportation, established parks, recreational areas, and jobs. Massive oaks, willows, maple trees, established lawns, hearty hydrangeas, and gardens invited new homeowners to the area.

The house was a sturdy model from the mid-sixties that the previous owners had started to update. The taupe-colored, wood siding was solid. In a breath of fresh air, the owners had replaced the roof with the insurance money they'd received after the last big storm.

I had bid on the house at auction and bought it for a sum firmly under market price. It was a contradiction in the economy. Cheap housing, but with no jobs, who could afford even a cheap house? Now, besides a list of rehab projects, I was in a quandary about why and how a dead body was in my attic.

After much angst during our ten-minute wait, Myra and I greeted the sheriff on the stoop. I led him through the entry, walking on drop cloths, past paint buckets to the step ladder under the attic access tucked in the main floor coat closet. The attic, where we'd found the dead man, was part of the weatherization and insulation aspect of rehabbing the house.

"I would think the inspector would have seen a body in the attic," I whined to sheriff Don Williams, as he climbed the ladder, stretching his long, muscular body through the access panel in the closet. In one graceful movement, he hoisted himself up to a sitting position on the edge of the loft's opening.

I caught Myra watching the sheriff's acrobatics with a coy smile. She flashed me an innocent, 'who me?' glance with an irrepressible sparkle in her eye.

"He would have, if the body had been here."

"Aww, jeez."

My mind raced back to the auction while the sheriff stepped down the ladder.

"You mean, someone could have left him here after the inspection? I've been painting and cleaning, and all that time he's been here?" The thought made me a little panicky, and I could hear a hint of hysteria in my voice.

"Can't say. We'll know more after we get the results from the medical examiner's report." The sheriff's cool, blue eyes held mine for a moment longer than felt comfortable. Don Williams was taller than average, with a little stockiness that said he liked a good meal. He exuded a masculinity that said he liked women.

Oh, and no wedding ring. Not all men wear rings, and not every man wearing a ring, wears it well. You've seen those guys twisting their rings.

I'd met the sheriff at a couple of foreclosure auctions before buying the solid, ranch-style house. He had intense, clear blue eyes. The fact that a ring was absent made those cobalt-colored eyes inviting, and much more interesting.

At that moment, I was covered in dust. My jaw was tense and set in its stubborn position. My hair was uncontrollable as I'd forgone the latest goo from the beauty supply store that promised to tame hair. I wore a gray sweatshirt with the logo of a tourist location from a long-ago trip with Jake, faded blue jeans, and tennis shoes.

Self-consciously I brushed back my dark mane, cursing my appearance, as the sheriff talked. I attempted to focus. After all, I was single. And, although I had a corpse in the attic, I hadn't killed the man.

"Now, what do I do?" I knew I wouldn't like my options.

"Now, Katelyn," he spoke deliberately, "we'll have to close the house while our crime scene investigators process the house."

"Perfect." I sighed, and winced. The time frame to recoup my investment just got a whole lot longer. "For how long?"

"We'll let you know," he said in a measured tone. He glanced over at Myra where she stood beside me. Her expression was impassive, except for one arched brow.

"Any chance the guy wanted a place to crash? And the door was open?" I ventured, a glimmer of hope.

"Won't know anything until the medical examiner sees the body." His voice was firm.

"Okay." It was a long shot.

"Say, didn't they just demo that house across the street last week?" he asked, and removed his hat. Silver strands of hair shined against blond locks, as he idly rubbed his head, then settled his cap.

"They did," I said. The local fire department had done a controlled burn the Friday before as part of a training exercise for the firefighters. The bright-red fire engine and firefighters had distracted me from my work. I had been painting one of the bedrooms and shut the windows to stem the wafting odor of smoke. I had been frustrated with paint from a discount store, because instead of the usual two coats, it had taken three coats with the primer, to get the paint color right.

"Oh, yow! Maybe he was dead and left in the wrong house?" I asked, and gasped. The idea seemed incredulous, but no more so than where the body was now.

"Seems like it could be a clever way to get rid of something somebody didn't want," he said. "Except firefighters search buildings before they do a training burn."

"Oh," I said. "Guess not." I was searching for a quick solution. Something that would put my life back on track. Fast. It didn't look like that would happen.

The sheriff stared me down. About to leave, he said, "I can't discuss this with you. It's an open investigation. Don't touch anything. I'll get back to you."

As he headed outside, I couldn't help but notice his muscular build under his uniform. Myra and I exchanged glances, and I fluttered my eyelashes in our private joke. He glanced back, narrowly missing our expressions, adding, "You'll have to vacate the premises while my people do their work." We followed him outdoors to the cool fresh air. Pausing, on our way to my car, we saw that the sheriff's department had already taped off the outside of the house.

We watched the activity in front of the Bluebird Street house while seated in my latest jalopy, a faded green, Ford station wagon. I'd bought the car at a salvage yard, thinking it would come in handy for hauling supplies. I was still finding its quirks. After running out of gas with a gauge that said half full, I now watched the odometer closely. I'd replaced a dented hood that wouldn't latch, and carried an open box of baking soda in the back-seat to eliminate stale cigarette odor. Myra, bless her soul, never smoked a day in her life but didn't complain about the residual scent. Myra had been silent while I talked to the sheriff. Now, she appeared as discouraged as I felt. "The bright spot in this mess, is that it doesn't appear the sheriff thinks you had anything to do with this," she offered.

"I'm not so sure about that," I muttered, remembering how the sheriff's eyes panned over me while he studied my face.

We kept watch as the crime scene people went in and out of the house.

I sensed Myra was feeling somewhat responsible for the sour direction, this "change your life, and follow your bliss mode" had taken.

"What kind of mess did I get myself into?" I murmured. I wasn't trained in crime solving. Just nosy, with a steely determination and plucky persistence to get to the bottom of this predicament.

Myra and I inhaled deeply, as two of the sheriff's people toted a gurney out the front door. I shuddered, and a chill went up my back. Seeing the body on a stretcher in daylight made it all too real. I started the car, maneuvering into traffic past gawking neighbors. I couldn't watch anymore.

"Sorry," Myra said, adding, "What a mess."

"Not your fault," I answered.

"I can float you a loan. It'll take time to sort all this out."

"Thanks, Myra." I sighed. "I'll be okay."

I drove Myra to her lake home nestled in the heart of the city. Minneapolis has a three-lake chain of lakes in the area. Her home overlooked the "couple's lake" as it was called by residents. Another was known as the "single's" lake; the third was branded the "family" lake.

Her home dripped elegance. It was a colonial style with dormers and classic shutters that set off red brick. The grounds were newly mowed with lush green grass that resembled a soft velvet fabric. Topiary bushes were groomed to represent different shapes of animals, birds, and a pair of deer.

I was out of my element driving my economy cars up the steep winding driveway next to the stately home. It never appeared to bother Myra getting out of one of my clunkers.

"We'll be in touch," Myra said, giving the car door an extra shove as it didn't catch the first time.

"I'm sure of it," I said, and watched Myra stroll to her front door. Her entry door was decked out with an immense spring-themed wreath adorned with daisies, twigs, greenery, and a large decorative bow.

I made the tight turn in the driveway, coasting back onto the parkway along the lake and waved goodbye.

Little did I know how soon, and where, we would meet next.

CHAPTER 2

The next morning, I sat at my kitchen table studying my checkbook, wearing my standard uniform of sweatshirt and blue jeans before leaving to check on the house. I sipped a cup of strong Colombian coffee and calculated my balance. It wasn't pretty.

Chewing my bottom lip, I pondered getting one of those survival jobs that I'd taken to get through college. I was starting to question my sanity about telling my old boss that hell no, I wasn't going to be a file clerk.

My phone rang, and before I could say 'hello,' Myra asked, "How are you?"

"Peachy," I lied, and tugged a bill from the stack next to the checkbook.

"That good, huh?" Myra could always tell from the tone of my voice if I was telling the truth. Another reason she and I are friends.

"Outside of needing a job selling widgets until I can get to work on my house, and this dead body thing is figured out, I'm fine," I insisted, bracing myself for what Myra would say. Sure enough, it came—a light rebuke. "I told you I could float you a loan."

"You know that saying about lending money to friends? How it makes problems for people. And how you shouldn't lend money to friends or relatives, unless you consider it a gift?"

"Yes..."

"I wouldn't take money from friends or family, unless I was dead. Then, I wouldn't need it." I bit my bottom lip and stopped, hearing how gruff I sounded. I was relieved when after a long pause, I heard Myra's laugh.

"Okay," she said, chuckling.

"I know, I know, it's silly. But I don't like owing people anything. In particular, money," I added, tossing the electric bill aside.

"That's okay. Just remember it's an option," she said, trying to soothe my ruffled temper.

"Thanks. I'd better go." I gave a sigh of relief as I hung up. I cursed the damned work ethic I'd been raised with. An ethic I shared with Myra. I'd rather eat peanut butter sandwiches for months than admit I needed a loan. But the checkbook was saying cut back on something, anything.

Myra and I had met a dozen years ago, at a local home improvement store during a Do-It-Yourself class. I was a fresh-faced, twenty-three-year-old, newly divorced from my high school boyfriend, bad boy Eddy. I hadn't met Jake yet.

The workshop was on faux finishing. Her rag-rolling technique appeared to be the professional deal.

"Eek," I said, as I stood back, observing the panel with my technique. It was as if someone left their toddler to clean the wall with a dirty rag.

"Eek," as I studied the result.

Myra turned to me with a tight smile, saying in a cultured voice, "It's all about the proper lighting."

"Oh sure," I countered. "Maybe no light at all would be the best presentation."

She burst out laughing. "You have spunk," she said, sizing me up.

"Maybe spunk, but no talent for this." I wanted to add texture and dimension to my walls, without hanging wallpaper, like the class promised.

"Perhaps color is more your thing," Myra suggested, adding, "You can add texture to a room with different patterns and materials in furnishings and carpeting. There's another class on selecting colors after this. How about joining me?"

"Yeah, that might work, because this is downright pathetic." Thus, our friendship was born. I think Myra saw me as a project. I reminded her of a younger Myra. She thought she could tame the undisciplined, messy side of me. If she only knew.

During DIY classes, I learned more about Myra. She was a home economics teacher in a local high school. Her husband, Marvin, held a safe, unexciting job as an accountant in the state's tax collection's department.

Myra's father had owned a construction company; construction was part of her DNA.

Marvin was an heir to the owners of the oldest and largest department store in town.

Myra and Marvin resided in an affluent section of town, but appeared to live a low-key existence with extraordinary wealth. Despite her wealth, Myra seemed just as happy to meet at a diner as at the country club. Not that I had any affiliation with country clubs.

Six months after Jake and I married, Myra lost Marvin. Myra and Marvin's conscientious attention to finances, along with a multi-million-dollar life insurance policy left her comfortable.

When Jake was killed in a car accident, we were just starting out and never thought about financial security. I needed a job. Myra, not so much. She brought her sense of money and value. I brought courage, or maybe foolishness, to the table. It was my money, my house.

Myra is also home-renovation addicted and tolerates my touch of paranoia. She is my biggest cheerleader in following my passion to redo houses.

From the get go, I admired Myra for her eye for detail and ability to analyze any situation. She had the experience and vision to know market trends and what would lure a buyer. She held a real estate sales license and encouraged me to get licensed too. It's on my 'to do' list.

"Buy the worst house in the best neighborhood, if you're going to make this work."

"What are you—channeling Martha Stewart?" I asked. In fact, she resembled Martha somewhat, with a rosy complexion and golden highlights in her hair. Now at fifty-five, her perfectly styled do framed a face of someone who could be mistaken for a younger woman.

"How about we call you a Home Renovation Specialist?" she said, with a twinkle in her eye, and a mischievous smile.

"Ooh, classy."

My phone rang again.

"I need you to come in to the station to give your statement." Sheriff Don was curt and to the point. The little thrill I'd felt when I heard his voice receded.

"When?"

"Now!"

"I'm on my way." The receiver clicked in my ear. I shrugged, uneasy at his terseness. Most of my interactions with the sheriff had been warmly cordial. He'd seemed sincere and solidly behind my efforts to renovate houses.

"Owner occupied homes help the neighborhood. Abandoned houses are a blight and a magnet for crime," he'd said, when I bought the house on Bluebird. He offered me his card and said, "If there's anything I can do, don't hesitate to call." I'd been on a high, excited about getting my first project, and accepted his card, noting how warm his hand was.

I slipped out of my grungy work clothes, grabbed a shirt I'd worn earlier in the week, scrutinized it, and satisfied, pulled it over my head. I slipped into black slacks, my staple for any occasion where jeans didn't work. That included seeing the sheriff.

I headed to the bathroom, splashed cold water on my face, brushed my teeth, threw on makeup, and combed my hair. In another stroke of genetics, I had gotten Dad's bushy hair. Dark brown, thick, and unmanageable. I needed a haircut. But, a haircut, like a lot of things, would have to wait until I could get my project house sold or rented. As I considered renting out the house, *Great, I really could be a slumlord.* Shuddering at the idea, I added another layer of hairspray to calm my frizzy do.

I threw on a black blazer, grabbed my handbag from a chair at my kitchen table/desk, and dashed out the door. As I drove the few miles past the strip mall that held a

McDonalds, an Asian restaurant, and a variety store, I considered being a landlord.

There's nothing wrong with being a landlord. Lots of people do it. The house I was fixing up was far from a slum dwelling. Nonetheless, I was pretty sure I would be a terrible landlord. I'd let any tenant with a bad luck story take a pass on paying the rent. I'm a mush for hard luck stories. With a bohemian mother married to a drill sergeant father, my childhood was full of hard times. Neither could fix the other and I spent my youth navigating a land mine of fights. I got out at sixteen, and vowed I would never live my life in a combat area again.

That promise faded when I married Eddy and we created our own war zone. Our passion was hot, but our tempers were hotter. That marriage lasted a year until Eddy took up with a bimbo, whose name I've conveniently forgotten. I nursed my wounds by redecorating my apartment. Eddy drifted in and out of my life until I met Jake. Jake was a calmer, steadier mate.

My life was headed in a positive direction.

Then Jake died.

Eddy found out and wanted to start things up again. I wasn't having it.

By this time, I was a homeowner. That's when I threw myself into painting, staining, and other home projects. If I couldn't control events outside of my environment, at least I could control my home's surroundings. It wasn't rocket science.

I turned off the main drag at the corner where the Crocus Heights Bank anchors the intersection. The police station was in the old downtown of Crocus

Heights, a first ring suburb of Minneapolis. There's a diner, a caterer, and a corner bar within a block of the station. The drive took all of about ten minutes.

My wagon makes a 'barroom, barroom,' sound when I start or shut off the ignition. It's an intermittent noise and fixing it has low priority. I crank up the radio, set it to Country Western to drown out any sounds of impending car repairs. Besides, I like the loud music. Toby Keith's tune, "Should've Been a Cowboy," was blaring from the radio as I parked and switched off the engine in the lot across the street from the police department.

I hustled out, grabbing my handbag. Standing tall, squaring my shoulders, I crossed the street for my meeting with the sheriff.

I was ready for battle.

CHAPTER 3

My courage fizzled as I sat outside the sheriff's office, taking in the photos of the mayor and city council members prominently displayed over the water cooler—two women and two men. Beside the mayor's portrait, was a picture of the sheriff in his uniform. His smile was broad and the twinkle in his eye apparent.

I squirmed in my chair, while cooling my heels for nearly an hour. I felt like a truant waiting for the principal. Once I'd misbehaved to the point of being sent to the principal's office. I'd mouthed off to a teacher on the playground. Maybe this wasn't so different.

Finally, I heard Sheriff Don's muffled voice and the phone receiver being replaced, signaling he'd just hung up from a caller. He leaned around the doorway of his cluttered office and motioned me in. Easing his body into his chair, he glanced at a piece of paper on his desk. I perched on the edge of a wooden chair across from him.

He straightened, faced me, leaned back against his chair, and studied my face. I felt the tension in the air as he said, "Ms. Baxter, we have identified the gentleman's body found on your premises yesterday. How do you know Mr. Jimmy Woo?"

"Jimmy Who?" I drew a blank, ignoring his tone and formal greeting.

"Woo."

"Woo, who?"

"Not funny, Ms. Baxter," he said, glaring.

"You're right. It isn't funny. But I don't know any Jimmy Woo." I searched through my memory bank for a glimmer of name recognition. I got nothing.

"You've never had any contact with a man by the name of Jimmy Woo?" His expression was skeptical, one that said, 'go on—make my day, tell me another lie.'

"No." I shook my head, "Why?"

"Woo was a patient at Colossal Health (oops, the sheriff named my former employer) where you were last gainfully employed," he snapped.

"Gainfully employed," struck a nerve, and I blurted, "I don't know what you are implying, Sheriff Williams, but the hospital is a huge conglomerate." Taking a breath, "I had no direct patient contact, and as far as work goes, I am now GAINFULLY employed as a home renovator as you know." I was on the defensive, and it made me sound guilty. Okay, I was a little sensitive about that employed part.

"Ms. Baxter, a second body was found in another foreclosed home," Sheriff Don said, interrupting my rant.

The expression on my face appeared to settle the sheriff's mind about something.

"Where?" I demanded.

"In the crawl space of a split-level home about two blocks from your house. Same deal. The house closed the week before. The new homeowner was cleaning up from the prior occupants. He opened the access panel to the space under the stairwell, and—bingo—another body."

I was shocked. Not only because another body had been found, but because I knew the house Sheriff Don was talking about. It was one I'd bid on. It was a nice house, only needed cosmetic work. Good use of space. Nice wood-burning fireplace that could be used as is or converted to a natural gas unit. It had a fenced-in yard with loads of mature trees. Someone could make a decent profit on fixing it up.

Another buyer had come in with a better price, and by default I bid on my traditional ranch that needed more work, but was still affordable.

"Who owns the house?" As soon as I spoke, I realized how damning that sounded.

Sheriff Don straightened in his chair, inspected me with his deep blue eyes, which were fringed by the longest eyelashes I'd ever seen on a man. He arched one eyebrow and rubbed his temple.

"Now, Ms. Baxter, I think you know why I'm asking all these questions. Possession is nine-tenths of the law. The person in possession of the body, usually knows so-o-omething." He drew out his last word in a drawl.

Suddenly, I didn't like the sheriff's appearance as much. I didn't like what he implied, and I had just thrown suspicion on another hapless homeowner, like myself.

"I know how it looks, Sheriff, but I assure you I had nothing to do with Jimmy Woo's deceased body in my house. I do not like where you are going with these questions. If I am not being charged with a crime, I am going to leave. If, for some reason, I am being charg…"

Sputtering, I stopped myself in mid-word. "I want a lawyer!" I stormed, getting up, adding, "I want my house back!"

"No need to get your shorts in a bunch, Ms. Baxter," the sheriff said. "You'll get your house back in due time. Just don't leave town." He gave me a smug smile and a searching gaze.

I felt my face burn as I flounced out of the sheriff's office, and I nearly tripped over Myra in the chair I was in earlier.

"They called you?" I gasped.

Myra's expression was blank, mixed with resignation. It said to me, "I am so mad I could spit." I'd seen that same look when a workman had dropped a hammer on her newly installed teak flooring, and dented the wood.

"They're just doing their job, Kate."

I snorted, still angry, in a hushed tone. "If they were doing their job, they'd be out searching for the person, or people, who did this!"

"Ahem. You can come in now, Myra. Ms. Baxter was just leaving."

The sheriff stood stiffly at the door to his office. My guess was he'd overheard everything I'd said to Myra. His manner was kindlier for her interrogation.

"How's your brother?" he asked, as she rose to enter his office. Myra's brother was the county's police chief. The sheriff had done his homework, he'd discovered that the Myra at my Bluebird rehab house was the chief's sister. It was clear he knew she wasn't involved in the body in my attic. Me, he wasn't so sure about.

"He's well, Sheriff. I'll tell him you asked." She pivoted towards me and whispered, "I'll call you, later."

I was aggravated Myra had been dragged into this mess. I hated myself for thinking the sheriff handsome minutes earlier, but I was still grateful he didn't consider Myra a suspect.

When Myra entered the sheriff's office, her jacket, matching slacks, and coordinated blouse showed off a trim figure and had just the right amount of class required for an interrogation by the sheriff.

I felt frumpy in black, carrying my oversized handbag. A quick glance at my reflection in the glass side panels of the door confirmed it. My attempt at smoothing out my mop just added to my overall dowdiness.

But, thankfully one of us—namely Myra—could stay calm in the face of a storm. My shorts were seriously twisted.

On my way home from meeting with the sheriff, I stopped at the Bluebird Street house. Yellow crime scene tape stretched across the front door. "Why me? Why my house?" I muttered. And then I sighed, "Why not me? Why not this house?"

The house was like many others built in the sixties, a low-profile rambler, with red brick facing adorning the front. It was a deluxe model, ahead of its time with an attached, single car garage. It was a simple home, built without the several stalls that today's homes often boast.

The home was sturdy stock with original hardwood floors. One of the features was a clothes chute in the hall between the bedrooms. Built with two bedrooms, the dining room was through a separate door off the kitchen.

It was often used as a third bedroom or nursery for young families, as the galley-style kitchen left enough room at one end for a kitchen table and chairs.

The basement was partially finished with a washer and dryer in the basement, painted walls, and carpeted floors. The open ceiling showed floor joists and ductwork. One large room was sectioned off with a door, but without a closet for storage. It could be a teenager's hangout. Most people today would call it a starter home. I guess that's why it called to me. The house promised a fresh start. Something that could be fixed, made anew.

On impulse, I drove around the neighborhood, searching out the second house where another body had been left in the basement crawl space. The house the Sheriff Don told me about in his interrogation. I had to be sure it was the same house I had bid on, and I was more than a little curious, i.e., nosy.

More crime scene tape cordoned off the split-level entry. It was deserted, and appeared as if investigators had processed the scene and left. It was another cute, starter house. But its market value had declined with the discovery of a body, like mine.

"People don't like to buy houses with sad events attached to them. They want happy houses," I could hear Myra saying, even as I gunned the motor and drove home, a saner, safer sanctuary.

CHAPTER 4

I live in a townhouse in the same area where Jake and I lived as a married couple. Our home held too many memories. I sold it for a decent profit and paid cash for my new place. I wanted simple, but with a bit of space. Let someone else shovel the drive and mow the lawn. I wanted the luxury of coming home from work and not fretting about yard work. A few pots of flowers in the summer and an occasional house plant—those that thrive without fuss, and sometimes water, are good.

My roommate is an indifferent stray cat that I named Boots for his white feet. With black fur and white markings, he appears to be sporting a tuxedo. He yowled outside my patio door last fall, desperate to get out of the rain. I'm not a cat person. I like dogs. But I opened a can of tuna, put it in a bowl, and opened the door. He darted in, devoured the fish, and meowed for more. He's made himself at home, and I haven't had the heart to tell him that I prefer dogs.

We've forged a relationship where I feed him and give him the run of the house. I'm gone a lot. He seems satisfied with the arrangement and stays on. If he belongs to another human, he hasn't told me. I haven't seen his face on any posters people put up in the neighborhood when their beloved pets go missing.

When I came through the door, he greeted me with a sniff of disdain and sauntered back to where he slept, tail held high. I shrugged out of my jacket and hung it in the hall closet.

"I can always trade you in for a dog," I warned the cat. He reconsidered his greeting and circled back to rub his body against my legs, purring.

"That's better." I stroked him, and put out dry food. He smelled it and stalked off. He prefers canned food. At least, that's what I make of it. Boots undoubtedly has his own version.

My new home and pet suited me. Low maintenance.

If it's a fact of life that the shoemaker's children go barefoot and the carpenter's house is in disrepair, my home showed the results of 'work in process.'

I'd moved in nearly a year ago, and although my bedroom is a sanctuary, the place desperately needs a personal touch. The kitchen table is my office, complete with a computer and printer. The walls are barren of art. All my personal photos and mementos are packed away. A few boxes are stored in the living room in one corner, awaiting attention. Other boxes are stowed out of sight, in the spare room. My plan was to paint before I unpacked. I hadn't quite gotten to it.

At first, it was because I couldn't come to terms with making a home for myself without Jake. Then, after my unfortunate incident with Colossal Health, I came home exhausted from finding the Bluebird Street house and starting the renovations.

I went to the refrigerator and grabbed a snack, then crashed on my sofa. Boots watched me with more interest when he saw the piece of leftover Hawaiian pizza from the previous night's dinner in my hand.

"No," I said, and frowned. He scurried to his favorite spot on the back of the sofa. Once there, he fixed his steady stare on my lunch, waiting for a crumb.

My home had come by way of my housing fix-it consultant and repairman, Wayne Hamer. I found him through the "handyman" want ads in the local paper when I began to consider flipping properties. He's a semi-retired carpenter who told me about the unit for sale, a foreclosure in his building. He lives in the end unit, and a corridor connects all four homes. The development is tucked away in a private wooded area. Built some twenty years earlier, the complex has elbow room. The lot is filled with mature spruce, maple, and oak trees.

The location and appearance of the complex attracted me. It was close to parks if I wanted to take up serious exercise—which I've managed to avoid most of my life, and handy to a coffee shop to fuel my caffeine addiction.

The four-unit building resembles an English Tudor-style house with cream-colored stucco. Dark wooden beams accent the peak of the roof line. It doesn't have the sterile multi-unit housing appearance of most townhome construction. It looks like a home. Most importantly, it had been affordable. It was a bank-owned property.

The unit I bought had been occupied by an elderly woman and her son. The son was a ne'er do-well and when his mother passed on, stopped paying on the modest two-bedroom unit. Well, you know the rest.

It was clean, but needed cosmetic touches, new carpet, and fresh paint. The master has a full bath, and another bath serves a small bedroom and guests. I call the second bedroom the spare room. I'm not sure what I will use this area for. A guest room seems presumptuous, as I don't have many visitors. I have a low tolerance for roommates, male or female.

For now, the extra room stores unused furniture and more packed boxes. In the back of my mind, I'll make the room an office, but for now, my kitchen table works just fine.

There is a wood-burning fireplace—which I intend to make gas-burning as soon as possible. It may seem romantic to throw a log of wood on the fire, but again in the interest of low maintenance, throwing a switch to start the fire is more romantic. Not to mention hauling wood, starting the fire, and cleaning the fireplace.

The tiny kitchen suits me, as my inclination to cook matches my ability to cook gourmet meals, hence the leftover pizza for lunch.

I've kept my expenses down in keeping with what happened with Jake and the crumbling economy, but I did need an income. I'd have to solve this dilemma sooner, rather than later, to keep a roof over my head and food on the table. I couldn't afford to wait until law enforcement found the culprit responsible for leaving dead bodies in vacant houses. I needed to get my Bluebird Street house renovated and sold. The sooner, the better.

"Rat a tat-tat!" came a knock at my door. The sound meant Wayne had seen my car in my parking stall.

"Hi!" He grinned impishly through thin, silver metal rimmed glasses with round lenses. Wayne was a self-described, left-over hippie, favoring an eyeglass style reminiscent of John Lennon, an old rock star. He was about six-feet-tall with a wiry, athletic physique honed by years of construction work.

With a little imagination, and lots of know-how, Wayne could transform a piece of wood into an elegant piece of molding. His knowledge and expertise with construction and carpentry was a God-send. He could take out walls that no one would have known were there, giving a house a fresh style. He was equally adept at changing out plumbing fixtures. He worked cheap, supplementing a social security check. He had a few devoted clients, and worked by referral with a no-frills business card that was made with a printer and construction paper.

He was a great craftsman, but not so good at marketing. I would offer to bring him up to speed, except for the guilty knowledge that that would garner him more jobs, and he wouldn't be as available for my work. He had a daughter in Michigan he visited over the holidays.

"Myra called, and told me about your newest occupant in the Bluebird Street house. A real stiff!" He threw back his gray, pony-tailed head, and guffawed. Wayne had a gallows kind of humor. It took a little getting used to. I'd come to accept it as part of his view of life.

"It isn't funny, Wayne. The police think I had something to do with it. They might bring you in to question." I stepped into the hall and grimaced, adding, "After all, you've been doing the work at the house for me!"

"No kidding. Bring it on," he said and chortled. He wiped tears of laughter from his eyes. "I'm sorry, kiddo."

Wayne always called me kiddo. In deference to my being thirty years younger, even though I was his employer.

Sobering up, he asked, "What do the cops think happened?"

"I don't know. All I know is I got the drill about 'Don't leave town without letting us know' from Sheriff Williams," I said, and rolled my eyes.

Like clockwork, the door to the unit next to mine opened. Mrs. Gilman, another retired resident in the complex, entered the corridor. She held a letter in her hand, ready for the mailbox at the end of the driveway. A quiet woman, she had the uncanny knack for opening her door whenever I had any company.

"Yo! Gillie!" Wayne flirted. "What's up?" Smiling broadly, he greeted the small woman. Mrs. Gilman had been a widow for several years. Wayne told me her husband, Walter, had been a big man whose booming voice had overshadowed his wife in social situations. She was private. Lately, I'd seen her taking walks and puttering around the patio of her town home.

The winter months keep most people indoors. As the weather warms up, people migrate outside. Mrs. Gilman was no exception. She was trim and still attractive. No doubt she was a beauty as a young woman.

"Hello, Wayne, Katelyn." Mrs. Gilman nodded as she passed us. Mrs. Gilman did have a first name, Greta. I saw it on a letter once. I never felt comfortable enough to use it. She always used Katelyn, avoiding my nickname, Kate, which most people favored. Her cheeks reddened, as Wayne's warm smile rested on her face.

"You look very nice today, Gillie." Wayne grinned and lowered his eyes to her bright, coral-colored hoodie and matching sweat pants. She appeared to be dressed for another long walk in the neighborhood or for working with her plants.

"Thank you, Wayne," she said, giving him a shy smile. Her short hair was styled in a pixie cut, and colored a strawberry blonde to hide the natural light gray. Mrs. Gilman was fortunate to have a pretty gray colored hair. If I was lucky enough to get the same hue at her age, I would keep it natural. But who knows what color I'll have with this curly mass of dark hair?

We smiled at Mrs. Gilman. I motioned Wayne into the vestibule after he finished watching her disappear from view. He still grinned, but didn't quite cat call. He pursed his lips as if it were a habit hard to break from years on construction sites, when calls to passing women were expected from the crew.

Wayne stepped into my unit and I shut the door behind him. He gave a low whistle. "I like what you've done with the place," he said dryly. It had been a while since Wayne had been in my house. We tended to have our business meetings at the job site or at a nearby coffee shop.

"Okay, okay. I've been a little busy."

"So, I hear."

"Sheriff Don said another body was found in the split level on Cardinal Street. It was a house I saw before I bought the rambler on Bluebird."

"No kidding," he said, and clucked. "This is getting to be a nasty habit. And they got no idea about how this is going down?"

"Nope, nothing, nada, as far as I know," I said. "Except the person was hospitalized by the same medical facility I worked at."

"You don't say!" Wayne exclaimed, "Colossal Health? Guess I'm not going to put that place down as my first choice for medical treatment," he said, and chortled.

At that point, my telephone rang. Caller ID said it was Myra. She lost no time in greeting, saying, "Come quick to the Bluebird house; the police are releasing the house to the owner!"

I hung up, faced Wayne, and said, my breath catching, "Myra says to hurry back, the police are surrendering the house."

"I'll come with you! I'll follow you in Matilda!"

Wayne had named his white van, Matilda. It was a hefty, workhorse type of van, with a black grill and black trim. The type of vehicle that would keep running past its usual life span. I'm sure when Wayne christened the vehicle, he meant no offense to anyone with the name.

"Thanks, Wayne." I was grateful for his company. I'd never found a body in a house, had the house closed by the police, and then released. The current situation seemed unreal and a bit scary. No, it was a lot scary.

CHAPTER 5

We raced to the parking lot where Matilda and my economy ride were parked. I say 'economy,' because my budget said 'cheap used,' and the cars I drove reflected that price point. It stood out next to the sleek, white, Jaguar convertible owned by our newest resident, Ariel Kominski.

Wayne and I stopped running when we spotted Ariel. Her long arms were wrapped around her new beau in the parking lot. She was a big, blonde-haired woman, à la Anna Nicole Smith. Like some large women, she had a babyish voice and was unaware she wore clothes more suitable for a teenager. She appeared to be in her late-twenties, a few years younger than myself. On this day, she wore a ruffled, low-cut blouse that showed off ample cleavage. A chain with a silver cross was nestled in the crease between the "sisters" of her cleavage.

"Hi, Wayne. Hi, Kate," she trilled in a breathy tone. She was about to get into the driver's side of her car when her keys slipped through her fingers. She reached for them with long tapered fingers, the nails brightly polished. The leggings that completed her outfit resembled a worn pair of pantyhose, a fashion trend I passed on. Leggings are not pants.

She giggled as she picked up the keys, taking a few seconds longer than I deemed necessary, giving the man with her a huge smile and a show of her full bust line as she straightened. I clutched my spring jacket a little tighter.

"This is my boyfriend, Paul," she said, and motioned towards him, giggling again.

Paul was at least six inches shorter than Ariel. He had a permanent smirk, giving him the appearance of a small-time thug. The image was completed by a dark swarthy face, and black hair slicked back into a duck tail. His attitude projected arrogance mingled with smugness. He slipped on gold, aviator-style sunglasses as he slid in the passenger's side of the white Jaguar.

Ariel giggled again as she got behind the wheel of the flashy car and put on big pink plastic-rimmed sunglasses. Besides gaudy, I recognized the logo as a designer of a line known as "luxury."

"Hi and bye!" Ariel yelled, as she gunned the engine and waved, dismissing us, and driving away, her new boyfriend slouching in the passenger's bucket seat.

"Hi, indeed," Wayne sniffed, and chuckled. "I know that look. How do you suppose she got that car?" He had a gleam in his eye, asked, "How high can we go?" and snorted.

"Nice outfit," I commented, my eyebrows raised.

Wayne smirked.

Ariel was a puzzle. She worked a regular job as a bank teller, yet drove extravagantly expensive vehicles. The unit she lived in was the same as the others in our building.

My first contact with Ariel had been on garbage pick-up day when I took out an empty pizza box.

She'd given a condescending glare to my grease-stained box, and sniffed at my "hi." She drew herself up to her six-foot model height and said in a self-righteous tone, her nose wrinkled, "I eat fruits and vegetables. Salads and fish. Healthy food."

"Does pineapple on pizza count as a fruit serving?" I had asked, kidding, on the fateful trip to the garbage bin.

Ariel had scowled at me and said, "My mother is wealthy and my father is an attorney. They own a line of grocery stores." She sniffed, adding, "My ex owned the Fitness Salons. It's a chain of work-out shops." As she went on and on about her moneyed background, I tuned her out. I guessed she sensed how little that meant to me, because eventually she turned up her nose and strode away. I observed that the heft of her body and her diet claims didn't match. And, why would someone with all that money and connections work in a bank?

She had moved into the complex in early spring driving the Jaguar with a license plate that started with WJ. The plate had a white background that caught my attention, and puzzled me. I pointed it out to Wayne.

"Whiskey Junction!" he chortled, with a knowing smirk.

"What's that?" I asked.

"It's a license plate for someone with a DUI violation. Driving under the influence," he drawled. "Can't say I haven't known a drinker or two, or three," he winked. Wayne had had a problem with alcohol that he freely admitted. If there was anything more, he kept it to himself. He had beat his addiction with the popular twelve-step program, Alcoholics Anonymous, and was very public about his antics as a free-wheeling youthful alcoholic and, I suspected, druggie.

"Yep, I just never got caught," he said, and added, "not by the cops, anyways. The wife got plenty fed up, though." I learned in one of our late-night sessions rehabbing the house that his wife had left him. She'd taken their daughter to Michigan, her home state. That was his wake-up call and he got sober, but it came too late to save the marriage. She decided to stay in Michigan and raise their daughter with her parents.

"Biggest regret I have, never raising that kid of mine," he said, showing a paternal side that didn't surprise me. He called me "kiddo" after all.

"I think Ariel's ex-husband had money." I shrugged, changing the subject. "Her family is wealthy, too."

"Uh huh," Wayne said, skeptically.

"Ariel told me her mother had bought the Jaguar as a present when she graduated from some on-line degree program," I said absently. "She was quite open about having money on both sides of her family. Good for her."

She had told me all this in our fateful food conversation on garbage day. Information I personally would never divulge to a neighbor in a casual conversation—even if true and I had the good fortune of a moneyed background.

"Uh huh; we should all be rich," he laughed.

I could only ponder the mystery of how some people were born into families with money or married into money, and how some toiled their entire lives to make a living. Okay, I get annoyed with people who don't recognize their gifts.

Could the news of the dead occupant in my rehab project have reached Ariel? Could she possibly have something to do with the body's appearance in the attic?

I nixed the thought. She and Paul appeared too comfortable to have spent time moving a dead body. Wayne pulled up in front of the rambler and I came to a quick stop just behind his van. When we got to her house, Myra was waiting at the door, appearing first class, wearing a black fleece warm-up jacket, black jeans, and a scarf draped around her neck.

Myra has the inside track on what happens at police headquarters with her brother as the chief of police. She'd entertained me on more than one occasion with tales of how he'd kept another drug dealing scum ball off the streets. I entertained her with stories of Eddy, miserable dates, and finding and marrying Jake. In between, we traded opinions on the perfect color and brand of paint, the pros, and cons of laminate versus wood flooring, and the latest home design project.

"Glad to see you, Wayne," Myra said, nodding at us as we approached. "Sheriff Don called my brother to let him know they finished the investigation," Myra said. "They've bagged all the relevant samples and they couldn't keep the house hostage after they were done. The crime appears to be leaving a dead body on the premises. They are taking down the crime scene tape this morning."

"What ever happened to notifying the homeowner?" I asked, grumbling.

"Oh, I'm sure he tried to reach you. I just got the information, shall we say, a little ahead of the curve?"

Myra said, and winked. "There they are." Myra wore a polite genteel smile for Sheriff Don as he strode up the walkway with another uniformed officer.

"Good to see you again, Myra," Sheriff Don greeted her with a smile, eyes twinkling. "Always a pleasure talking to the chief."

"He'll be happy to hear that," Myra said pleasantly. I thought I might barf.

"What's the scoop, Sheriff?" I asked.

"The crime scene investigators are finished with the house. The medical examiner says the man died from injuries sustained prior to being relocated to your house's attic."

"Really?" I asked, nonplussed. "That's what the coroner said? Relocated?"

"Really, Ms. Baxter," Sheriff Don said, holding my eyes with his very blue ones again, "Mr. Jimmy Woo, or JW as he was called, was a patient at the time of his death. He died from injuries sustained from blunt force trauma."

"Why was he in my attic?"

"That's the mystery, Ms. Baxter," Sheriff Don responded dryly.

"Blunt force trauma? That means, he was hit by an object?"

"I'll be in touch," he said. "Remember, stay close to home, Ms. Baxter."

"What does that mean?" my voice raised an octave.

"Just what I said," he countered. "We may have more questions." The sheriff looked perturbed, and I backed off. Ticking off law enforcement wasn't the best idea. I wasn't going to be traveling anyway. But it bothered me I was told not to, even if I hadn't planned on it. He couldn't possibly think I had anything to do with this, could he? I gulped, fearful that I could be a suspect in this escapade.

Another officer cut yellow tape and wrapped it into a ball, disposing it in a black plastic bag. A wave of relief washed over me as the remnants of tape disappeared into the sack.

The sheriff got in the squad car along with his deputy and drove away. I watched them leave, irritated by Sheriff's Don admonition to stay close to home. Was that a hint he thought I was involved?

If the past week hadn't tainted the home's market value, I could have it sold along with a tidy profit by autumn. The thought that my house could be on the market in time for summer home shoppers after all, softened the blow of the sheriff's suspicion and cheered me up.

CHAPTER 6

Wayne and I redoubled our efforts at fixing up the house. I completed all the painting inside. Wayne finished spraying the attic with foam insulation, changed out bathroom faucets and framed out the bathroom mirror to hide flawed silver backing. It looked like a new mirror when he was finished.

With a little shudder and a prayer, Wayne closed up the attic. Myra and I readied ourselves for our first open house. I didn't have the funds to rent furniture and accessories to stage the home, so I concentrated on cleaning. My furnishings were sparse, with a beige card table and two matching, metal folding chairs.

We sat at the table the first day of the showing with color brochures and specs on the house. It was the second Sunday following the crime scene tape removal. We'd needed every minute of the full week, plus a day to finish the house.

The first couple that entered had a young toddler in tow. They were young, hip, and tough. The man wore a gray, nondescript tee shirt and distressed blue jeans. The woman wore similar clothing except for a tee shirt with a motorcycle logo. Both wore silver wedding bands.

"Where was the stiff found?" the young woman demanded. She wore a metal stud through a piercing in her right eyebrow. It would hurt like heck if she caught the earing with a flick of her hand. Her hair was short and spiky, colored blue, and her son's hair was the same style with blue streaks.

She plucked up the advertising piece and stood, glaring down at me, while I sat at the card table. Slowly, Myra and I rose to face her. She was eye level with me and maintained her stance, her attitude challenging.

"Hush, not in front of the boy." The man scooped up the toddler. He disappeared with the boy struggling in his arms into a back bedroom. I heard the boy saying, "I want Mommy," in a high-pitched whine.

"Where was it?" she demanded. "I wouldn't want to buy a house with bad karma. Even if it was cheap!"

"Affordable," I countered. Myra and I locked eyes with one another. We were prepared to deal with a buyer's right to know and full disclosure of the history of the house, just not this quickly. The man hadn't been murdered in the house, so we didn't have a legal obligation to disclose the death, but possibly a moral one.

"The man didn't die in the home. He was found in an unused area of the house," Myra said. We would do our best to downplay the details. Especially, since it appeared this woman was more interested in drama than buying a home.

"Huh? That's just plain crazy. He didn't die here?" she demanded, snorting.

"It's complicated," I said, tensing under her glare.

"Well, where was he? If he didn't die here, then someone put him here," she countered. "Maybe you, huh?"

"Like I said, it's complicated. The police are investigating," I offered, my arms wrapped around my midsection in a standoff. And at the same time, trying to reassure her.

"The body wasn't found in the main living areas of the home—the kitchen, bathroom, living room, and so forth," Myra piped in.

"Oh, you mean he was in the basement, or something?" the woman asked. Scanning the brochure, she glanced from me to Myra as she skimmed the information.

"But I want Mommy!" her little boy yelled.

The young man emerged from the bedroom exasperated, carrying the boy, whose crying escalated to shrieks. "We'll be in the car," the man threw out as he left the house. The boy let out another screech, both arms flung out at his mother. She appeared oblivious, while she shot another question at us.

"Was it the basement?" she asked. My body tensed again, and I bit my lip, distracted by the twitch of the woman's eyebrow.

"No," Myra said, stepping in. She repeated, slowly, teeth clenched, "The body was not in the main living spaces of the house—kitchen, bedrooms, living room or bath."

"I don't want to be doing laundry with a ghost watching me!" Disgusted, she threw the brochure on the card table, shook her head, and followed her husband out of the house. Myra sat down, and each of us let out a sigh of relief after they disappeared.

"We should have just told her," I said, and gave a moan.

"It wouldn't have mattered," Myra said. "How do you think she'd have felt about hanging her coat in a closet with the attic access?"

"She would have a ghost watching her every time she hung up a coat," I said, giggling.

Myra joined in, chuckling.

"Yeah," I conceded. "You're right. What am I going to do if this house doesn't sell?"

"It'll sell. It has good bones. Oops," she gasped, and said, "I didn't mean it that way."

"I know what you meant."

After all, it was a solid little house in a decent neighborhood, close to shopping, parks, and amenities at a steal of a price—just like the brochure advertised.

Two small, brown-haired women who resembled each other, entered the house within a few minutes of the first couple's departure. Myra and I smiled at the pair as they entered. The older of the two walked slowly beside the other. Each carried a tissue and wiped at tears threatening to run from dark eyes.

"Are you the owner?" the younger one asked Myra.

"She is." Myra gestured to me with a tight smile. This was going to be another difficult conversation. She ducked and started to leave the table, and I placed my hand on her arm to stop her. She sat down.

"How can I help you? Do you have any questions about the home?" I asked. I was wary. These women looked tired and didn't appear as if they were shopping for a house. In the back of my mind I heard, *never presume anyone's financial state from their appearance.* Many people with money don't advertise it. Often, the wealthiest among us live frugally to avoid unwanted attention. Both women had fatigue clinging to their faces and their clothing was worn. Okay, I was reaching.

"Jimmy was my son!" the older woman shouted. Myra jumped, and I flinched.

"Quiet, Mama! You said you weren't going to make any problems," the younger woman chided, resting her hand on her mother's shoulder.

"Quiet, quiet?" the older woman asked. "That was my Jimmy in this house! How?" Her wild eyes fixed on my face. "Why? You look like nice lady—why was my boy found in your attic?" Then, she muttered something in a voice too low for me to catch.

She's probably putting a curse on me, I thought with a sinking feeling.

She ended her discourse in a hushed whisper, "Jimmy hit by car!"

"Ma'am, I am truly sorry about your loss. The police are conducting a full investigation," I answered, with what I hoped was a tone of sincerity.

"Bah!" she countered, spitting in a low voice.

Now, I'm doomed.

She turned and ambled to the living room's picture window, where she paused and gazed out at the street.

"You'll have to excuse my mother," the younger woman said, adding softly, "She wanted to see where my brother, Jimmy, was found. You know, to pay our respects. We couldn't afford a real funeral. Mr. Randal said his burial was paid for by the county."

"That funeral director, Mr. Randal, said we don't pay for Jimmy's funeral. He'd take care of my Jimmy, no worries!" Jimmy's mother blurted out as she returned to our table. Directing the tirade at her daughter, she fanned herself.

"Do you want to sit down?" I asked, and started to get a chair, worried if she would make it out of the house.

"No!" the woman retorted, and moaned. She opened her eyes, and stopped cooling herself.

I paused, and the younger woman said, "Our family couldn't afford a funeral. Mr. Randal, he owned the funeral home. He said the county would pay for burial, but no service or viewing, just a coffin and a plot," Jimmy's sister explained. "It would've been enough. It was a shock to the family he was found here."

Jimmy's mother shook her head. She had calmed down, wandered to the entry, and departed the house. Jimmy's sister glared at Myra and me.

"Again, I'm so sorry for your loss," I said, wilting under her stare. "The police would have any information on the investigation."

"Yes, ma'am," Jimmy's sister attitude softened. "It's a real nice house," she added. "You painted pretty colors. If things had been different, maybe Jimmy would have had a fine house like this one."

"Thank you."

"Jimmy had problems. He got into drugs and that was the death of him."

"Your mother said he was hit by a car?" I asked.

"Our family thinks he was running from his drug dealer. He owed the man money."

"Oh."

"The drug lord hit him with his car. He tried to make it look like an accident."

"What makes you think it wasn't an accident?"

"Jimmy was on the sidewalk when he was found. There were tire tread marks on the grass by his head. That meant the driver drove off the street and killed him. They never found the person responsible. The police said it was a hit and run."

"Why do you think it was a drug dealer who hit him? It could have been anyone."

"Jimmy was scared. He asked me to lend him money to pay off his debt. Told me the guy would kill him. He was dead the same day."

"I see."

Myra and I murmured more condolences as the younger woman headed to the exit.

"We didn't mean to cause any problem." She glanced at us, about to leave. "If you hear anything, we would appreciate it if you would let us know," she said. "Good day, ma'am," she said and left, letting the door slam behind her.

"We're done for today," I said, turning to Myra, exhausted.

"Amen to that," she agreed and we gathered our brochures.

"Do you think it was too soon for an open house after finding Jimmy's body?" I asked.

"Maybe," she murmured, as she stacked the flyers, and handed them to me.

"People need a little bit of time, another event to focus on, so that they can forget," I added, putting the leaflets into my bag.

"You may be correct," she said, nodding.

"What will I do?" I muttered. The sunny day had changed to overcast and cloudy along with my prospects for getting the house sold.

"Let's meet at Popov's for dinner to celebrate the first showing," Myra suggested. "The house is done. People will forget. It will sell."

What Myra wants, Myra gets.

CHAPTER 7

Popov's is our hangout to celebrate, commiserate or just get together. It's owned by Russian immigrants, Ivan and his wife, Maggie. Ivan is there every day chatting it up with customers. Rumors have long swirled with the locals that the establishment has ties to drugs and illegal activities. If there were any such dealings, I was unaware. We were there for the food and drinks. Sometimes we drank coffee, other times something stronger. We could always count on plenty of refills and being left alone for our extended conversations.

The burgers are big and nowhere near healthy. If I'm in the mood to watch calories, I'll have a light beer, diet coke or black coffee. We go during happy hour for wine on special occasions.

That day, we cooled our heels in a small booth off to one side of the restaurant which was filled with people having Sunday dinner. I ordered black coffee. Popov's portions were supersized; coffee was no exception. I cradled the mug of hot java and watched the crowd.

Quietly, Myra sipped lemon ginger tea from a large white mug.

After the harried waitress dropped off our food and dashed off to take other diners' orders, we hunkered down, munching on burgers and fries.

"What a day! What did you think of the first couple?" I asked, breaking the silence, and sighing as I added, "the woman who didn't want bad karma? The woman with the pierced eyebrow and blue hair?"

"Unbelievable. It was quite a day," Myra said, pausing to take a sip of her drink. "Oh, and after that, Jimmy's relatives walk in. How about that scene?" she asked, and groaned.

I snorted in agreement, took a bite of my burger, chewed, and swallowed, reflecting on the day's events. Idly, I picked at a fry. After taking a gulp of coffee, I mused, "Maybe we need an exorcism or something?"

"Huh?" Myra stared at me. "You are kidding, aren't you?" Panic etched across her face. She knew me well enough to sense trouble when she heard it.

"Uh uh." I shook my head.

"What on earth do you mean?" Myra asked, frowning.

"I mean, not a full-blown exorcism, but some sort of ritual to cleanse the space." The thought had nagged at me after the open house, while I hung out with Boots at home. I'd spent the time surfing the web, trying not to fret about the lack of a buyer. Most realtors will tell you that open houses are a dicey lot. It is possible a buyer can come from a showing, but not always.

Cleansing the space could renew the area. If I hadn't yet solved the mystery of how and why Jimmy Woo had appeared in my attic, at least I could eliminate any negative vibes from his presence, while I worked on finding the culprit or culprits.

"I don't know of any priest or minister who would do such a thing—not that it isn't done," Myra added in her cultured voice, shrugging. "I'm not into that sort of thing."

"Why couldn't we do it?" I asked. The do-it-yourselfer in me rose to the occasion. "The day Jake and his friends helped me move, one of the guys told me to break a glass against a wall in my old apartment. It was to clear the space for the next occupant. Break with my old life, to usher in my new life with Jake," I explained.

"Really?" Myra looked at me skeptically.

"Yeah. It was symbolic; out with the old—in with the new."

"I guess it couldn't hurt," Myra said, considering my suggestion. "What would we do? Break a glass in the attic?"

"There are other rituals. I just happened to look them up." While distracting myself that afternoon from my budget, I had researched cleansing rituals on the information source for everything and anything—Mr. Google.

"Well, okay," Myra sputtered. She was trapped.

"Let me tell you what I found," I said, inspired.

"Oh, me." Myra gazed at me like I'd lost my mind. She is practical. If it looked, walked, and quacked like a duck, it was a duck. She didn't go in for the unseen, otherworld, kooky, spooky stuff. I was the one with the bohemian mother and a quirky sense that not everything has a physical, practical explanation. I like to think there is a greater meaning to my life than I see sometimes. There may not be, but I'd like to think so.

Like Myra said, a ritual to get rid of any residual karma couldn't hurt. People want a happy house, a fresh house. A cleansing ritual couldn't hurt, could it? It could change our luck. I was getting psyched thinking about it.

"There's a bunch of them—but this one appears doable," I said as I dug out my notes from my handbag.

"Oh, boy." Myra clasped her hand to her forehead, like someone getting a migraine. It could have been the tea, but I doubted it.

"It looks pretty simple," I went on, enthused. "You get dried herbs, like lavender and mug wort, and light them," I went on. "They suggest using a candle to light the herbs. Then, blow the smoke into areas where negative energy may linger. The smoke sucks out the adverse karma. The bundled herbs are called smudge sticks."

Myra winced, as she asked, "And, where do you get mug wort or lavender? For that matter, what is mug wort? This isn't witchcraft, is it?"

"Umm, no. It isn't witchcraft. It's a Native American cleansing ritual," I said, adding, "According to the web, mug wort is an herb."

"Maybe you can get lavender and mug wort at a farmer's market?" she suggested, visibly relieved I wasn't asking her to join a coven.

"I think so. But there are specialty shops," I said, and did my best imitation of a spooky movie introduction, "You know. Doo doo doo, doo doo doo?"

"Oh no," Myra protested. "You are not going to get me in one of those places."

"Uh huh."

"No. No way," she said, shaking her head.

I kept focusing on Myra's face while she protested, until she exclaimed, "Oh, all right!"

"It'll be fun," I chirped, adding, "We won't stay long. There's a place not far from here. I'll drive."

"No, that's okay. I'll follow you. I might have to leave in a hurry," Myra said, and sighing, took a sip of her tea.

"It'll be fun. It might even work." I nodded my head, trying to convince myself along with Myra. *Anything I can do to get this house sold; I will do.*

The shop was listed in the white pages in an area of Minneapolis called Hiptown. It's a part of the city best described as funky. Populated with students and what might be called "counterculture," its quirky shops catered to a diverse population. The big box stores had been kept at bay by the area's residents.

I parallel parked my Escort four car spaces from the Mystic Palace entrance and watched for Myra. More vehicles left while I waited, and she scored a parking spot next to the door. Already, good karma was with us. She smiled, resigned, her lips pressed together as we met outside the shop. I held the door, and she entered first while door chimes announced our presence. To the left as we entered, crystals were displayed on shelves along with books on the Tarot and other alternative religions. Soft music played in the background. We hesitated as our eyes adjusted to the dim lighting.

I sniffed the air. A woody scent, probably sandalwood incense, greeted us. I glanced at Myra. Her face was devoid of expression.

"Yep, this is the right place," I said confidently.

"Can we just get the dang stuff, and go?" Myra whispered, sniffing the air, her eyebrows raised in consternation.

"Can I help you ladies find something?" a mellow voice came from behind, as we gazed around the store.

"I'm interested in a smudge stick," I said, sounding nonchalant, as if it were another trip to the grocery store.

"Ah yes. From the Native American ritual of cleansing," the man's voice came smoothly.

"You'll find what you need over there," and he waved us toward a rack of incense sticks and dried bundles of herbs.

"Told you so," I said, smirking at Myra.

"Could we make this quick?" Myra asked under her breath, gritting her teeth. Her face was impassive as she noted the curious appearance of the man behind the counter. His white hair was long, flowing, and full, as though it had been blow-dried. It draped across his shoulders and down his back. He wore small round, gold-rimmed glasses perched on the end of his nose.

"Is there anything else we need?" I teased Myra. "A spell to attract love—or in my case, wealth?"

"Don't be funny. Get the danged smudge stick, already," she whispered, her voice tense, "This is creeping me out."

"Okay, okay." I picked out a bundle and examined it. I hoped this was what the ritual required. I didn't want to go home, reread the procedure, and find I hadn't gotten the proper item. Who knew what would happen if we used the wrong herb?

"I don't see lavender," I murmured to Myra. I put the herb bundle back, reading the shelf labels. "There's sage, white sage, and cedar. No mug wort either." I viewed the man behind the counter, absorbed in his computer screen, ignoring us. I picked up a printed description card for each bundle. "They all pretty much say the same," I said, scanning the information.

"That means they work the same," she hissed. "Can we get on with it?"

"I'll get one of each."

"Sounds like a good idea," she muttered and rolled her eyes.

"Along with incense, we got it covered," I said, smiling, satisfied I had found the solution to getting my house sold.

"But, of course, we do."

"Hey, this is serious stuff. We want any negative energy from Jimmy banished so I get a great offer on the house."

"All right, already." Myra's face was a mask of steely stoicism as a pair of young men with gauged ear lobes, their sleeveless shirts exposing tattoos, strolled past us. Myra cringed as they viewed us, paying special attention to Myra with her flawless hair, make up, and coordinated designer outfit. One of the young men stared at the diamond earrings Myra was fond of wearing.

"Okay, let's go." I went up to the counter, paid cash for the items and snagged a brochure on readings given at the shop.

"Do you want a proper shopping bag for these?" the silky-voiced man asked, as he handed me change.

"Yes. Please." I took the plain brown paper bag and stuffed in the leaflets.

"May you use the smudge with good intentions and it has the desired effect," the man intoned, smiling at us as we left.

"Thanks," I said.

"How do I let myself get roped into these things?" Myra said, groaning, outside the shop.

"Hey, you said yourself, it couldn't hurt and it might help. We have the best of intentions."

"I guess," Myra muttered.

"How about we do this before the next open house? I'll call you to set it up." I had a few days before our next showing.

"Sounds good," she said.

First, I had to make some money. Boots needed chow.

CHAPTER 8

The next morning, I studied my bank balance over a mug of rich, black Colombian coffee. It was time to do something, fast. Although, the body was out of my house, I hadn't heard anything further on the investigation. I had to keep a roof over my head while I sold the house, and got to the bottom of the dead body mystery.

With that in mind, I considered survival jobs in the local shopper. My best bet for a low commitment, cash opportunity in this week's paper was marketing research, or a sample person for a wine distributor. I considered my checkbook and comfort zone, and decided to do both.

The ad for the wine and beer distributor caught my attention: People wanted to host wine samples for a major manufacturer in metro liquor stores. Short term, weekends, and some weekday hours. Bingo, that could be me. I liked wine. I called on it.

After an introduction, came the big questions, "Are you twenty-one?"

"Heck, yeah."

"What hours are you available?"

"I'm pretty flexible," I said, crossing my fingers, hoping the hours they wanted wouldn't interfere with my new career as a part-time sleuth and home renovator.

"Bring a photo ID along with your social security card and we'll get you started," the woman said. "How about nine o'clock Monday morning?"

"Perfect."

"Multiple streams of income," I imagined Myra saying, approvingly. I wouldn't tell her of my plans because that would result in another offer of a loan I wouldn't accept. Yeah, I know. "Pride goeth before a fall."

Next, I called market research companies for openings.

I scored a couple of interviews—one with a research company at a nearby mall. Another, with a telephone research company, which assured me it wasn't a telemarketing company. "Of course, you make more if you set up an in-person interview," a sweet-voiced young woman added.

I set up an interview with the mall research company for later in the day. The telephone research company was doing group interviews another day. It depended on how the mall interview went, whether I'd go the telephone route. From past experience, I knew it was harder for people to blow you off in person, as opposed to hanging up before you said "survey." There was only so much rejection I could take.

Beat by the morning's activities, I put on another pot of coffee. The weather was nice enough to take my cup to my patio table, outside the kitchen slider. I sat, and savored the strong brew, feeling the coffee warm my veins. My addiction to coffee started young, and over the years I've worn out my share of coffeemakers. There is nothing like holding a strong cup of java to get my motor going. Boots followed me, basking in the rays of sun and a warm breeze.

My ears perked up at the sounds of a man and a woman's voice in the end townhome unit. Ariel's patio door was open. *She must be home for lunch.*

I inhaled, taking a deep whiff of air, enjoying the smells of spring. I sniffed again. My nose wrinkled at the combination of petrol and smoke. Not strong, but still apparent.

The voices from Ariel's townhouse became louder.

"Oooooh." I heard a woman's moan. It was Ariel's high pitched breathy tone. Another deeper voice, "Yeah, baby." Another long-drawn-out moan, "OOOhhh," ending in a whimper. "Oh yeah, baby, bring it on," a man crooned and grunted.

"Oh, great," I said to Boots. "Noon hour sex." The cat appeared to grin in agreement. He licked his paws and cleaned his face with his mitts. I heard the thud of Mrs. Gilman's patio door shutting. The sounds had likely reached her.

"I agree," I said, looking at Boots sprawled out in a sun-warmed spot on the brick pavers. "Are you coming?"

I went inside. Boots followed when he heard the refrigerator door open, and I gave him a treat from a pouch stored in the fridge. I closed the patio door, leaving a gap for fresh air. Sounds of Ariel and her visitor drifted through the crack in the door. I slammed the patio door.

It worked, and blocked the noise of Ariel's lunchtime activity.

"Good for her," I muttered to Boots, but I didn't care to hear them.

It was one o'clock in the afternoon. My interview at Mega Consumer Research was in an hour. Quickly, I ducked into the shower, covering my unruly hair with a shower cap. I had a new type of hairspray I was eager to use. It promised to keep my locks soft and manageable while holding the style.

I threw a black blazer over my black and white top, that matched my black slacks. Black was easy, not to mention slimming. I wore a lot of the color these days. I added a dab of cologne at my throat and wrists, slapped on make-up, and sprayed my hair.

"Not too shabby," I observed in the mirror. I'd answer my research questions.

I parked in the mall lot, entered the shopping center, and trekked down a semi-deserted hallway where offices were hidden from view of shoppers. I found the door for the Mega Consumer Research Group and walked in. An efficient receptionist handed me a clipboard with an application and asked me to take a seat and fill in the sheet of paper.

A minute later, while fishing my driver's license from my handbag, a young woman swooped in and sat down across from me.

"Hi, I'm Jennifer." She thrust out her hand.

"Katelyn Baxter." One hand was still in my purse, the other held the clipboard. I removed my hand from my handbag, and gripped hers. In the process, the purse's strap came off my shoulder and I let loose of the clipboard. She ignored the racket and pumped my hand until it went numb. After she released my hand, I gathered everything that skidded to the floor. My face burning, I sat up and faced her.

She had the air of an athlete. Energy and intensity radiated from her body. The set of her jaw and direct gaze reminded me of the no-nonsense attitude of Leona Helmsley, the wife of a hotel baron. She had been dubbed the 'Queen of Mean' by her staff. She micro-managed and browbeat the employees of her hotels, eventually going to jail for tax evasion. She famously said, "rich people didn't pay taxes; the little people did." When she died, she left her fortune to her dogs. The rich are different.

Jennifer was a young micro-manager in the making, with a firm jaw, deep green eyes, and long auburn hair. Her build showed many hours of honing a sculpted body displayed in a snug black dress. She wore three-inch heels adding to her commanding height. She appeared to be about twenty. I could be her mother, if her mother had started early. Okay, her mother's younger sister.

I'd just met her and knew I didn't want to mess with Jennifer.

"We want our researchers to be the best in the nation!" she trilled. She appeared as though her mind was on planet Jupiter while she went through her mantra. Although she exhibited professionalism, she could have been calculating her grocery list or next workout. "We demand top-notch people. And, you know what, Katelyn?" she assessed me eagerly.

"What?" I asked, meeting her gaze, my eyebrows raised. I briefly considered running. Then again, she could take me down in a minute.

"We GET the best! Our kind of researcher is thorough and excited about obtaining data from people. We want only quality responses from our consumers," she paused, taking a breath. "If you fit this profile, you could be a valuable team member of a LEADING research company! Isn't that exciting, Katelyn?"

"Oh yeah, exciting." I felt my blood pressure rise. I tried to sound enthusiastic, as I considered stopping shoppers on their way to their destinations and quizzing them about products.

Jennifer never hesitated during the remainder of her rehearsed speech. I gave the appropriate 'uh huhs' and nodded. My mouth was frozen in a smile. My eyes never left her face as she kept up her spiel, leafing through the script in front of her.

I sensed she was getting to the end of her prepared script when she took a breath and glanced at her notes. "We pay the full state minimum wage," she continued in her sing-song voice. "There are no benefits, as we do not require you to commit to full time hours. We expect you to be available most nights, weekends, and holiday hours for this amazing opportunity!" and she ended her drill.

I searched my brain, trying to remember what minimum wage was. It appeared Jennifer wasn't going to tell me.

"Katelyn, would you like to join our team of dedicated researchers? Your background in health care would be most valuable." She looked at me expectantly.

"Uh, sure."

"Great! I'll take a copy of your identification, driver's license, and social security card. We'll start training tomorrow!"

I considered my plans for the next day, my bank balance, and the stalled investigation. "Perfect," I said, and handed her my license and social security card. "Jennifer, what is minimum wage?" *Yikes.*

"Put me down for as many shifts as you need."

"Will do, Katelyn!" She gave me a tight, forced artificial smile.

I left the mall, glum, but relieved, reminding myself, *At least you can buy gas and food until the house sells.*

CHAPTER 9

I was shell-shocked from my interview with Jennifer, whom I quickly coined "Jennifer the Great." I needed a pick-me-up. The possibility of an opportunity to rehab another house always perked me up. For some women, it's new shoes; for me, it was houses. With that thought, I got into my car, and decided to visit a house that had caught my attention over the winter.

The house was a few blocks from my rehabbed house. I didn't have the money at the moment to pursue another project, but it didn't hurt to look. It was a little ranch-style house with weathered cedar siding. It displayed a masculine décor with a wagon wheel on each side of the front steps. A metal silhouette of a cowboy leaned at one corner of the detached garage.

The property was possibly abandoned, which was appealing—another prospect for my new occupation. Yellowing papers were stuffed into the box that held the local newspaper. An old, red pick-up with rusted doors sat in the driveway and hadn't budged from its position through the winter. There was a worn footpath to the back of the house between traces of crusted melting snow. Which meant the house must have been occupied through the long harsh winter.

On my trips to the Bluebird house, I had watched for any activity. Last fall, there was a man I presumed to be the owner working in the backyard, clearing a downed tree from one of our wicked storms. As Minnesotans are fond of saying, "If you don't like the weather, wait a minute, it'll change." We in the Midwest have a few quaint sayings.

He had a wiry build, and I guessed him to be in his fifties. His hair was long and wispy, brown, fading to gray. It hung down the back and sides of his head surrounding a shiny bald spot. A long gray beard completed a biker look, with a black leather vest over a red plaid shirt and faded jeans. Perhaps, he was going for a cowboy/biker appearance. He was always alone, which made me think he was a bachelor.

As winter wore on, the truck never moved, and I wondered if the house was vacant. I didn't see any smoke from the chimney and considered whether the owner had "expired" inside the home. By spring, the red pick-up remained in the driveway with all four tires flat.

With the ruckus in the neighborhood about the body found in my rehab house, I was more and more curious, as I hadn't seen any signs of life for several months.

After my interview with Jennifer, I was itching to get a closer look. I parked on the street a few car lengths from the house and switched off the engine, sat, and watched. Nothing, nada, no activity.

I got out of my car trying to appear nonchalant in case neighbors were watching. I bypassed the front steps and strolled the driveway past the derelict vehicle, to the rear of the house. The lawn was unkempt, but it was early for any serious yard clean-up. According to lawn gurus, it's never wise to start grooming a lawn too early. It damages the grass.

As I strolled, the sun warmed my back. I stopped to take in the lay of the backyard, which was hidden from street view. In one corner of the lot was a fenced-in area for a garden. The deer and rabbits in this area will destroy a garden in a heartbeat if it isn't enclosed. The appearance isn't desirable but the fence preserved produce grown in our short gardening period.

The back of the house held a screened-in porch. A rickety, wooden door blew open and shut with the wind. It must have been the main entry for the man I'd seen. My cursory view of the front entry staircase showed neglect with rotting wood.

Cautiously, I opened the screened door to the porch. The area was trashed. There were piles of black plastic garbage bags, empty cans of cola and beer, and stacks of dusty newspapers. The man was a hoarder, a disorganized one without a system for keeping stuff, instead saving everything—in contrast to hoarders who catalog and store their treasures in bins. I'd seen the phenomenon on cable television. Every episode made me want to clean out a drawer or cupboard.

A stench stopped me cold. *It couldn't be!*

The smell was coming from a corner of the porch. It smelled like a decaying animal— or something worse. I scrutinized the place where the nasty odor originated. I picked my way through the area cluttered with bags, boxes of discarded papers, and empty soup cans. The smell was stronger and more offensive. The garbage bags were yard waste sized, with enough room to dispose of a body.

I considered the possibility that the mess could hide the remains of someone who couldn't make it out of this maze, or someone who'd been abandoned like the body in my attic. Could the man who lived here be responsible for the bodies left in vacant houses? The hair on the back of my neck stood up. What if someone had fallen? I thought again of the man I'd seen earlier in the year cutting a tree into cords of wood. What if it was him?

I didn't like the sight or smell of the porch.

I seized my cell phone to dial 9-1-1.

The back-door burst open.

"Aaaack!" I shrieked. Gasping in shock, I whirled to face the man I'd seen working around the house. His stringy hair was wild and his face showed deep creases from sleep. He stood in the doorway to the house and gawked at me.

"I thought you were dead!" I blurted.

"Who are you?" he demanded.

He appeared harmless after the initial shock wore off. He wore the same outfit; a variation of the jeans, plaid shirt, and leather vest I'd seen him wearing about the grounds. Outside of his disheveled appearance, he looked disoriented from being wakened from a deep sleep by me, trespassing.

"I own the house a few blocks away that's up for sale," I said. "I hadn't seen any activity here for a while; your truck hasn't moved—so I got worried." I figured my best defense was a good offense, the concerned neighbor.

"You the woman who owns the house the body was found in?" He panned me up and down with a puzzled face, scratching the bald area on his head with thick, stubby fingers. "I seen you before."

"I am." I sighed. I may as well admit it. He wasn't a total hermit if he had heard about my house's unfortunate occupant.

"Look, lady. I don't like nobody nosing around my place. Least of all, somebody with dead bodies in their house." His sleepy, disoriented manner was replaced by disgust at my presence on his property.

"I'm sorry. Very sorry." About to leave, I hesitated, emboldened by my natural curiosity, and said, "There is a very unpleasant odor coming from that corner."

"Unpleasant, whew, stinks like a dead body," he snapped.

I winced, reminded of Jimmy Woo's body left in the attic of the Bluebird house. Thankfully, he hadn't been there very long.

"I dumped some broccoli there. Just plain forgot about it. Sun found it, now it smells like nobody's business. Got to get in there and get it out."

Spurred into action, he wove his way through the litter to the corner that smelled the worst. He stooped and plucked a box from beside a garbage bag filled to the bursting with debris. He held the container towards me as if to prove its contents. Both of us caught our breath, gagged, and twisted away from the offending smell.

Out of the corner of my eye, I saw the brownish-green stalks of what was once a vegetable. The box was full of several bunches of broccoli, now rotting waste.

"Satisfied, now?" he snapped.

"Sorry," I stammered, chastened. I pivoted and dashed from the porch to my car. As I left, I could hear the man grumbling to himself about nosy neighbors and how he longed for the good, old days. "Women stayed home, took care of the men, and people minded their own danged business."

Slamming my car door, I twisted the key in the ignition, giving the engine seconds to engage before I threw it in gear. Shuddering, I reflected on my encounter. The adventure had taken less than ten or fifteen minutes before I met up with Myra.

We were meeting for a late lunch at Popov's to brainstorm about what we could do better for our next showing, and I wanted to convince her we needed to cleanse the house—something this neighbor should consider on a different level—eek.

CHAPTER 10

Safe in a booth at Popov's, shaken from my adventure with the neighbor and the rotting broccoli, I held my coffee cup in an iron grip. "You wouldn't believe the day I've had," I said.

"Go on," Myra urged, "tell me all about it." Her presence calmed me and my blood pressure lowered to an acceptable level.

"For starters, I have a gig with the Mega Consumer Research Company. My new boss, Jennifer, is an Amazon—tall, redheaded, with a personality to match. She'll be a challenge."

"It's only temporary," Myra said, assuring me.

"I hope," I muttered.

"On the way, I made a detour past a house that could be a new rehab project. I wanted to take a closer look and meet the owner. Actually, he caught me trespassing on his back porch."

"You what?" she asked, her expression mesmerized.

"Yep, I was snooping, and smelled something horrid. It was rotting broccoli. For a moment, I thought I'd found a solution to my mystery. Maybe, the neighbor did it," I offered.

Myra chuckled.

"It smelled like someone could have died in the house," I protested, on the defensive. "Who knew rotting broccoli smelled like rotting flesh?"

"Makes one want to give up eating broccoli," Myra said, laughing.

"No kidding." I sighed, exasperated by my encounter with the neighbor. "At the very least, he could take in his papers, move his pick-up, and shovel his driveway in the winter. Take some pride in home ownership," I grumbled.

"It sounds like he might have fallen on hard times."

"I suppose," I conceded.

I changed the subject delicately. "When did you want to do the…ritual?"

"Oh, whenever it works out for you; I'm pretty available," Myra said. It was apparent she was hesitant about our foray into the other worldly realm. She was a little too casual in her response, but was resigned to the prospect, and didn't know how to bow out gracefully. She was going to humor me.

I was okay with that. I needed to be indulged. I was squeamish about the unseen, other worldly dimension. If it's unseen, we don't know if it really exists, do we?

"Okay," I agreed, "I'll have a break tomorrow afternoon."

"Sure," she said, and heaved a sigh.

While we kibitzed about the open house and went over the list of people who'd signed the register from the first one, I looked up from the guest list to see what was becoming a familiar sight, Sheriff Don. He brushed past our table on his way to another table following the hostess.

I'd know his back anywhere.

"Look." I nudged Myra and motioned towards Sheriff Don's table.

"Oh, how nice," Myra murmured.

By this time, we were wired on our third cup of coffee.

Sheriff Don studied his menu, but sensed we were watching. He turned towards us, put his menu down, got up, and strolled to our table. Secretly, I was flattered the sheriff would approach us in a social situation—without a dead body, that is. I braced myself for any sparring about my whereabouts in relation to the investigation.

"Hello; you ladies look like you're enjoying yourselves today," the sheriff said, his eyes fixed on Myra. With a broad smile, he appeared the most relaxed I'd ever seen him. Dang, he looked hot. He exuded a natural warmth and appeared to be well-rested and ready for a good meal. That's the time, if you've ever been around a man who's hungry, things can get downright nasty.

Drat Myra, looking younger than she was. Her complexion glowed, and she appeared happy and at ease, seeing the sheriff.

"How's your brother?" he asked Myra, glancing at me.

"Very well, Sheriff. I'll let him know you asked."

Sheriff Don beamed with Myra's comment and said, "Good."

He addressed me, saying, "I just got a report of a woman trespassing at a home not far from your house on Bluebird Street."

"Really?"

"You don't know anything about that, do you, Ms. Baxter?"

"Why do you ask?" I asked, evading the question.

"The neighbor who made the report resides in a house which is not well-maintained, and looks abandoned. Someone could be snooping around, thinking there was some connection with the Bluebird Street house investigation. Maybe, even searching for another dead body." Sheriff Don watched me; his expression serious.

"Really?" I felt my face do a slow burn as I met the sheriff's gaze.

"You don't want to be messing in police matters, Ms. Baxter," he reproached. Abruptly, "You ladies enjoy your coffee." With that, he gave me another quick once-over. I detected a touch of annoyance. *Oh yeah, I'm the snoop with a dead body in the attic. Oh, and no helpful brother in high public office.* I relaxed, relieved at his departure. There was a sparkle in his eye when he took one last gaze at Myra and me while he sat at his table. Or was it a tear? Maybe he was hungry and thinking about a great burger.

Myra interrupted my musings of Sheriff Don with a nudge to my elbow, "He is such a nice man. He'd be perfect for you, Kate. If you would just be nicer," she said with a coy smile.

"He wouldn't want anything to do with a Rehab Specialist." I'd just coined the title with new business cards in mind. "Renovation Specialist." My current title sounded soft. "Rehab" sounded snappy and quick.

"Nonsense. He'd be lucky to have a woman like you," she countered.

"He seems to find *you* charming," I answered. "Me, not so much, I'm a meddler."

"He's not my type," Myra said decisively.

"Really?" I asked, with a spark of hope. Myra had never admitted to having a type. Or any interest at all in men since her husband had passed, but one can never know.

"Been there, done that," she said firmly. It was as though she had read my mind. Maybe, just maybe …

I avoided looking at the sheriff as we paid our bill and left the restaurant.

In the parking lot, I suggested, "Maybe we should do the ritual the day before our next open? That way, it'll be fresh."

"Sure," she agreed.

I was pleased. I figured she just needed a little more time to adjust to the idea. She was on board.

CHAPTER 11

A question niggled at the back of my mind after leaving Myra. How did broccoli man know about my dead body? He wasn't a reader, based on the overflow in the box that held local newspapers. I drove to his house and parked on the street, my engine running.

I peered at the weathered house. A metal contraption caught my attention. Above and beyond the cowboy silhouette lawn art, at the far corner of the roof, sat an old-fashioned antenna. Broccoli man kept up with the neighborhood through television. The bodies and investigation *had* made the local news.

Sheriff Don's earlier comment about how convenient it would be to dispose of a body in a building slated for a controlled burn also rumbled in my mind. It was a good time to take a tour of the neighborhood where the other body had been left. Could there be some link to the training sites? Could a body be overlooked or hidden somehow? The sheriff had dismissed the thought, but I had to be sure.

As I cruised past my rehabbed house to the end of the double-long block, I spotted a sagging garage on a vacant lot. I lowered my window and studied the detached garage. The white paint was chipped and weathered. One end was supported by a two-by-four piece of lumber.

Sirens sounded in the distance. Then, the deep horn of a fire truck blared as it lumbered through the streets. I put my car in gear and headed towards the noise. I could have stayed put. The fire truck stopped in front of the failing garage.

I parked a safe distance behind the fire engine and watched as the firefighters hustled off the truck with water hoses. I don't know what came over me, but what I did next defies any reasonable explanation.

I plead temporary insanity.

I couldn't contain a feeling of dread as I observed the men prepare for the fire exercise. The feeling started in the pit of my stomach and welled up through my chest until I leaped out of my car and ran toward the garage, yelling, "Stop, stop!" at the top of my lungs.

The crew hesitated when they saw me. One man, whom I guessed was the fire chief, barked an order to the others to stop the session. He was massive. I guessed his height at about six-and-a-half feet, and his shoulders the width of a doorway.

The chief pivoted, towering over me in his uniform of khaki colored jacket with wide reflective yellow tape, yellow helmet, and khaki pants tucked inside brown rubber boots, and demanded, "What seems to be the problem?"

"There's a body in that building you're going to torch!" I yelled hoarsely, out of breath from my sprint. My belly and chest ached and I gasped, struggling to catch my breath.

"Stop work!" the chief yelled. The other firefighters stopped unloading equipment.

The chief stomped to the garage side door and looked inside. Satisfied, he twisted, glaring at me.

"Follow me," he ordered.

"Okay," I nodded and trailed him to the side door of the garage.

"Watch your step," he snapped, and spun towards me, surprisingly graceful for a large man. "Now, I want to know what this is about. What body and where?"

Standing inside the dimly lit structure, I saw it was empty and clear of any debris. I looked into the rafters above the garage, and saw … nothing. The chief glared at me, and asked suspiciously, "What's going on, lady?"

"Uh," I stammered, "well, there were two bodies found in this neighborhood, and when I saw the firefighters and the training exercise…"

"You thought we were burning bodies in buildings scheduled for training!" he barked.

It did sound incredible.

"Lady, you'd better get off this site, or I'll have you arrested for trespassing, spitting, interfering with a firefighting exercise, and anything else I can think of!" the beefy man growled.

"Okay, never mind," I muttered and left embarrassed, my head down and chin tucked in. I hoped the chief would forget my lapse in sanity, and none of the firefighters at the scene would remember a hysterical, bushy-haired woman. I heard the trainees grumble and the chief mutter, "loony public," as I slunk off to my car. It wasn't my best moment.

As I got in my car, my cell rang. I plucked the phone from my purse. "Where have you been?" Myra demanded. "They found another body!"

I raced over to meet her in the same neighborhood where my Bluebird house waited for a buyer. Sheriff Don Williams and Myra waited outside the entry of a rambler with light blue siding and detached garage, while two men removed the body.

"Whoever did this, left in a hurry. They must have been spooked by the patrol cars in the area," I overheard the sheriff say to Myra, adding, "The new owner discovered the body in the living room." I joined them on the sidewalk.

How sad, I thought as we watched the sheet-covered figure on the gurney. When the police loaded the form into the transport vehicle, the sheeting caught on the door. From my vantage point, beside Myra and the sheriff, I glimpsed an elderly white man dressed in a hospital gown. He was unshaven and looked rough.

Three bodies so far, and who knows how long this would go on? My house was within six-blocks of this latest body. If this wasn't solved soon, I'd never get my house sold, the neighborhood would suffer from the unsolved crimes. I'd be doing consumer research for the rest of my life. I blanched thinking about the showing scheduled for Sunday afternoon. Sheriff Don left and got into his patrol car, following the van.

"My brother called me. He thought I'd like to know right away," Myra confided. "I overheard the men say it was frigid in the house. Most likely to hold off the smell of decomposition."

"Oh boy," I said, glumly.

"You know; this isn't helping the resale value on your house."

"No kidding."

"Why are they using this neighborhood as a disposal area for these poor people?" Myra asked, adding, "It's not a terrible part of town, not like some areas."

"There must be some sort of connection," I speculated. "It could be familiar. The person or people responsible for leaving the bodies know how to get in and out fast, without causing any commotion. Maybe they live in the neighborhood?"

"Or work here," Myra suggested.

"Huh." I was skeptical. The neighborhood was mostly residential, with a couple of mom-and-pop stores. There wouldn't be many jobs to draw people. Residents would have to commute for work. This house was similar to other housing stock; it was a single-story with a detached garage, but met the fate of many homes during the recession. It was abandoned, likely after the owners found themselves under water in an overpriced housing market. After some cosmetic work, painting and clean up, it would be ready for new owners.

All and all, it was an attractive area, except for the recent rash of lifeless bodies. Trees were budding, tulips and daffodils were starting to bloom in the early spring. The house I'd flipped had new spring color in the front yard as well. Lush green grass was growing and bushes were filling out.

We were about to leave the premises, when Sheriff Don returned in his patrol car. We stopped at the edge of the lawn.

"Oh oh," I said, as he parked and lowered his window.

"Hello, Sheriff," Myra said. "Back, so soon?"

"Hello, Myra, Katelyn," his deep voice greeted us, a gleam in his eyes. He nodded and said, "Just got a call from the fire chief. Seems he's getting someone from the public at controlled burn sites looking for dead bodies. It's annoying. You don't want to annoy the fire chief."

He studied my face for any reaction.

"Do you have any leads in these cases?" I tried to keep my tone and expression neutral.

"I can't discuss it. It's an ongoing investigation," he said, adding with a rueful smile, "but, we can't have civilians playing investigator when we don't know what's behind this. It interferes with police work. You understand, Katelyn. It's my job."

"I understand," I said reluctantly. I felt warmer towards Sheriff Don. He redeemed himself for his interrogation about Jimmy's unfortunate appearance in my attic. And, he hadn't forced the episode with the fire chief. He drove away.

"He's such a nice man," Myra said, watching until he was out of sight.

"Uh huh," I said, sighing at the memory of Sheriff Don's broad shoulders. My mind snapped back to the present. I turned to Myra. "Do you think we should still have the open house this weekend?"

"It can't hurt. We have a house to sell," Myra said, her head high, chin out and determined. "We must show whoever is doing this, they're not going to scare off buyers or investors."

"Are you ready to do a cleansing?" I asked, watching her expression.

"Arrgh, all right," she said, with a grimace. "Let's do it. I'll meet you at the house."

"Great. I'm almost there." I jumped into my rusty Ford, eager to get on with the ritual.

CHAPTER 12

With my gut churning, nerves on edge, and excited about the cleansing, I headed to Bluebird Street. The smudge sticks were stuffed into my generous handbag, along with a lavender-scented candle I'd picked up at the mall.

I parked in the driveway, considering how to get the most from the ceremony. I was psyched, thrilled this could be the answer to dispelling negative karma, and selling the house. If Jimmy's mother had put a curse on me, maybe this could remove it. I hoped she'd been venting, perfectly understandable.

I unlocked the front door while Myra parked on the street in front of the house. She joined me on the stoop, giving me a tight smile and followed me into the house.

"Okay?" Myra asked, as we stopped in the entry, slipping off our shoes, "How does this work?"

"I'm not sure," I said, "Let's see what the directions say."

From my handbag on the counter, I dug out the candle along with the smudge.

I took the instructions from the package with the smudge stick.

"I think the first thing we need to do, is relax," I said, viewing Myra, who had nervously locked the door, and paced the length of the living room.

"Of course. Do you have any wine?" Myra stopped, and asked, her tone hopeful.

"No wine. How about tea?" I offered.

"What kind of ritual doesn't have wine?" Myra looked at me, stubbornly.

"The do-it-yourself kind. The kind of ritual without a priest involved." We were both on again, off again Catholics, so I knew I could kid her about religion.

"Any brandy?" she asked, adding, "That would be relaxing."

"No wine, and nothing stronger," I said. "But I do have instant coffee from the last time Wayne and I worked here. And real cups, not paper." I rummaged through the cupboard for the meager supplies I kept on hand for long days spent working at the house, and needing a caffeine fix.

"Aha, tea, I have green tea!" Victoriously, I held the box up for Myra's approval. It had been part of a health kick after hearing glowing reviews about the benefits of green tea. Another futile effort to kick my coffee addiction. After that debacle, I went back to coffee.

"I think we should begin by meditating with a cup of hot tea, and consider our intentions," I said, encouraged by my find.

"Oh boy," Myra said. She clutched her purse and jacket tighter to her body, as if cold. But the house wasn't cold. Sunlight streamed through the picture window and warmed the living room.

I popped a cup of water with a tea bag into the built-in microwave and hit the beverage button. While it heated, I searched drawers.

"Matches!" I chortled. They were left by Wayne who had no qualms about health issues and still smoked a pack a day. I gave Myra her tea and fixed the next cup for myself. "Sorry, no sugar or lemon."

"Uh huh, next cleansing we do, I'm bringing better refreshments." She started to relax, placed her purse next to mine, and removed her jacket, putting it in the crook of her arm. She was calm as she considered the house. "It's a great house, perfect for a young family."

"It is," and I sighed, following her gaze.

Taking my cup, I waved to the folding chairs set up in the living room. "Let's sit and meditate for a few minutes."

"But, of course." Myra draped her coat on the back of the metal chair, and settled into the chair, with her cup of tea.

Taking my cup and the information from the sage bundles, I sat in the chair facing her, shifting on the cool, metal seat, getting comfortable.

"This is serious stuff," I said. "Let's close our eyes and ponder what we want to accomplish today."

"Umm," Myra chanted and giggled.

"You aren't helping."

"I can't help it. It's how I get, when I'm losing it." She snickered again.

"It'll be fine," I assured her. "Get a grip."

We sat in silence, closing our eyes to contemplate our purpose.

"Okay," I murmured and opened my eyes after a few minutes. "Let's see what the directions say." I unfolded the slip of paper from the bundled sage. "It says to light the bundle and set it on a heat resistant plate, then let the smoke envelope your hands and body. My plates are paper—have to use another mug."

I rose and went to the cabinet, found a cup, and held it up proudly. It was a white relic with a logo of a plumbing company. I put the sage bundle in the cup.

"That will have to do." Myra wrinkled her nose, and picked up the instructions.

I brought the container to our chairs, and she summarized the directions, "Okay, it says, let the smoke drift over your body. Next, move the smudge through the house to cleanse and purify the areas of the home. Does that seem reasonable?"

"I guess. I think these rituals have to be somewhat flexible. Don't you?"

"This one does," she said, her brows raised.

I lit the lavender scented candle, and ignited the sage bundle with the candle. I presented the sage mug to Myra.

"Need another mug," I muttered, and nodded at the candle. With the candle in hand, I went to the cabinet, and found another mug, this one from an electrician. Placing the lit candle in the mug, I left it on the countertop and returned to my chair.

Myra and I looked at each other. She offered me the sage. I held my hands to the mug and the smoke drifted over my hands and face. I took the mug and moved it along my body. Myra did the same. We held our breath as the smoke curled.

"Okay," I said. "Let's start here, in the living room, go to the bedrooms, bathroom, and finish up in the kitchen."

"What about the basement?"

"Good point," I conceded. "We should start in the basement. We'll work our way upstairs to the bedrooms, bathroom, the kitchen, and finish with the attic access."

"We'd better get a move on. We'll run out of smudge," Myra said, getting up.

"We could," observing the bundle, adding, "I've got another one."

"Okay, let's go," she said, and led the way.

We descended the basement steps, taking care to keep the bundle lit. Letting the smoke drift around the walls, we strolled through the basement; the potential teen hangout, the main area, and ended at the laundry. As we came up the stairs, the bundle went out.

"I need more smudge." I went to the kitchen, took the other bundle from my purse, added it, and lit both. The bundles comingled in the mug and the stream of smoke thickened as it wafted out.

"Oh, this is good," I said.

We made the rounds on the main floor. At the edge of the attic, while smoke curled, I stopped and made the sign of the cross. Myra did the same.

I handed Myra the cup with the smoldering sage, moved a chair to the closet, and popped up the access panel. I took the cup from Myra and held the mug over my head to let the smoke drift and cleanse the attic where I'd found Jimmy's body.

"Schreeeeeeeeech!" I nearly dropped the mug when the smoke alarm in the hallway, next to the closet, went off. Myra jumped.

I quickly hopped down from the chair and handed Myra the smudge cup. She put it on the kitchen countertop, next to the mug with the lit candle.

"Oh, my god," I gasped. "That sounds hideous!" I placed the chair under the alarm, stood on the seat again, and reached for the release. It kept shrieking.

"Quick, open the windows, the door, anything!" I felt around the alarm's base, the noise was deafening. I twisted the cover, no dice.

Myra ran to a window. I jumped from the chair, making a detour to the kitchen, grabbed the smoking smudge, and ran to the door. I threw open the front door, letting in the fresh air, waving my free arm to clear the smoke.

"You again!" a big man bellowed and filled the doorway.

I jumped, gasping.

I looked up to the beefy face of the fire chief. He still wore his uniform, but had removed his helmet, which he grasped under one arm. His bulk was enormous and his attitude reeked of no-nonsense.

"Who called you?" I demanded.

"Your neighbor!" he roared. "He heard the alarm! He saw two women go in, heard the racket, and NO ONE came out."

"Where was this neighbor when they left the body here?" I grumbled under my breath.

"What?" The fire inspector barked.

"Nothing," I replied. "There's no fire. It was an accident. I got too close to the alarm with a…cup." And hid the mug, the sage now out, behind my back. I knew it sounded suspicious. When does a cup set off an alarm? The fire alarm had mercifully gone silent. Between the air from the windows and the open door, it had ceased its wail.

Myra popped in beside me with the mug that held the lavender-scented candle in her hand. "We were freshening the air from the stuffiness, before our next open house. Lavender can be such a wonderful scent," she enthused, holding up the cup. "The candle got a little too close to the alarm."

"Yeah," I added, "I meant candle."

The chief looked from Myra to me, and back to me.

"Huh! Might want to open a window next time," he grumped. "The whole danged truck and everything is outside. This is costing the taxpayers a bundle!" With that, he stalked away.

"Oh, we will, we will. We are so sorry," Myra trilled to his broad back. He continued his heavy-footed gait to the fire engine. I heard grumbling for the second time in a day, "Loony public."

I shut the door with a thud and collapsed against it. Leaning back, we gasped in relief and laughed hysterically. We heard the muffled whine and the motor revving on the fire truck as it sped away.

"That went well," Myra commented, as she wiped her eyes.

"Unbelievable," I croaked. "I think our work is done today," and dried my tears.

"You think?" Myra asked, gasping. Her snickers set me off again.

"Yeah, let's get out of here," I said, giggling.

In a burst of motion, we grabbed all the cups, emptied, washed them, snatched up our purses, slipped on shoes, and hurried out the front door.

"Let's not do this again," I joked as I locked up.

"Amen," Myra said, and nodded. "How about getting a bite to eat? My treat," she suggested.

"Thanks. I'm starving. The usual? Popov's?" I'd accept an occasional dinner from Myra without too much fuss. After all, we both had to eat. And it wasn't like she was handing me a check or a wad of cash.

"That'll work."

"I'll meet you there," I said, on the way to my car.

"Sounds good," Myra agreed, nodding as she opened the door to her SUV.

"Whew," I said as I slid into a booth at Popov's sighing. I was thankful to be away from the house. I leaned against the padded back of the booth. Myra relaxed in the seat across from me, and said, "Uh huh. It's been quite a day."

Warily, I looked around the restaurant to see if there was any sign of Sheriff Don. No sheriff. No fire chief. Life was good.

The place was busy as usual and an older woman, the manager, was filling in for wait staff. She dropped menus in front of us, her mouth pursed. She stood by, tapping her foot, waiting impatiently for our drink orders. We ordered coffee.

"I get you coffees," the brunette snapped, and pivoted. Popov's ran a tight ship, with a lot of turnover in wait staff. More than once, I'd seen a young trainee stalk off in anger, or leave crying after a few words with the woman or Ivan. We took the turmoil in stride. The burgers and strong coffee were to die for, and we were too preoccupied eating and talking to pay a lot of attention to the restaurant's drama.

That day was no exception; the rich coffee and comfort food was a balm after the day's escapade. The cranky brunette dropped off hot mugs of coffee, later plopped our plates of food in front of us, and vanished.

Diet was a four-letter word at times like these. My personal favorite was the Popov's burger—a huge burger with a special homemade sauce, two cheeses, bacon, tomato, and lettuce.

The nod to healthy was a blurb about sea salt on crispy fries. We were in heaven as we went over plans for the next open house.

"We can check cleansing off the list," Myra said, snagging a French fry and popping it into her mouth.

"Yep. Done. Clean as a whistle," I said, smiling confidently, and reached for my burger.

"Thank goodness," she said.

"Uh huh, amen!"

CHAPTER 13

The next morning, on my second cup of java, I went over plans for the next open house. On my third trip to the coffee pot, I took a break, mug in hand, and went to my patio window.

It was a beautiful day, a treat for a Minnesota spring. A light breeze beckoned me to open the slider and let in fresh air to banish stuffiness from the long winter. With the door open, I heard voices at Mrs. Gilman's patio. I knew the timbre of the man's voice. It was Wayne. He and Mrs. Gilman were deep in discussion over a dead rosebush.

"Don't worry, Gillie," Wayne said. "I'll dig it out for you."

"Oh, that would be wonderful, Wayne," she gushed. "You're so handy and so helpful."

Peering around the corner where the pair were huddled over the plant, I could swear Mrs. Gilman batted her eyelashes when she looked up at Wayne. Animated, with a rosy glow and wide smile, she wore another outfit of a mint green-colored hoodie and sweat pants.

Wayne grinned at her praise, "Glad to help out. How 'bout I go with you to the garden store to pick out a new rosebush, hon?"

I backed into my kitchen, embarrassed at eavesdropping on their private moment. Anyone who planted tea roses in this climate knew they were looking at a high maintenance, low reward kind of situation. Still, it was kind of cute seeing the two seniors flirt. Especially, the strait-laced Mrs. Gilman with Wayne, the left-over hippie. Opposites really do attract.

I carried my cup of coffee to the kitchen table, sat at the computer, and focused on the matter at hand. Getting my house sold was the first order of business. How bodies appeared randomly, not to mention why, in my neighborhood, was a huge priority.

What Jimmy's sister had reported about Mr. Randal taking care of her brother's burial troubled me. The conversation had nagged at me since the open house. It aroused my curiosity about the funeral home. I pondered what kind of system was in place for people who couldn't afford funerals?

I hazarded a guess. 'Randal' was part of the business name and so I checked the Google white pages for listings. Sure enough, there was a listing for Randal's Reswell Funeral Homes. I went to the webpage and Mr. Jackson Randal had first billing as the owner and mortician. I dialed the number.

"Randal's Reswell Funeral Home," a man answered on the first ring. His tone was smooth and practiced, "We're here in your time of need. How may we help?"

"I want to plan my aunt's funeral," I responded, thinking quickly. Surprised by a human voice, and not a recording.

"Has she passed?" the man asked, clucking in sympathy.

"No. She's in hospice," I fibbed.

"Certainly. This afternoon is open," he said. "After lunch?"

"I'll be there," and hung up before he could ask any more questions. The ruse was brilliant. But I wanted someone to come with me, male preferably—because, you never know. I wasn't going there under the most up-front circumstances. A fishing expedition could garner more information. Not to mention, I was a teensy bit apprehensive after my incident with the fire chief and the fire department. I wanted a plausible explanation for my meeting with Mr. Randal.

I busied myself with more research on the mortuary's services, and read they did "low cost" cremations. Satisfied I had all the information needed for a visit; I turned my attention to ideas for curb appeal for the next open house. Perhaps a pot of flowers, or new house numbers. New house numbers won out, when I considered travel and time to take care of outdoor potted plants.

Later, I looked out to see Mrs. Gilman watering and plucking a leaf from her new rosebush. Wayne was gone. I hoofed it down the hall to his door.

"Sure, kiddo. Sounds like a plan," Wayne said, grinning when I asked him to go to the mortuary. I had interrupted him putting finishing touches on a bookcase. Working with wood was a passion, as well as a career.

His home displayed expert carpentry skills with a custom fireplace mantel and built-in shelving. He had mounted crown molding in the living room, ripped out standard floor molding and put in a better grade. He'd removed all the wall-to-wall carpeting, and installed rich-looking, red oak, hardwood flooring throughout. It was definitely a masculine home. His off-hand comment when others complimented him on his work, was he had "woodified" it as much as possible.

In his retirement years, he had turned his love of craft to smaller commissioned projects, or gave custom items as gifts.

I didn't say anything about his earlier gardening activities with Mrs. Gilman, but marveled at the energy the man had.

"Sure thing, if you think it would help," he said, adding, "Sounds like fun! The sooner we figure out what's going on in this neighborhood, the better. Should I wear a sports coat?"

"You don't have to do that." I viewed his frayed jeans and blue denim work shirt. "Maybe a casual shirt and khakis? Business casual?" Seeing his latest project, I added, "I hope I'm not keeping you from anything?"

"Nope, just did the final coat of varnish," he replied, pointing with pride at the bookcase. "Going to give it to my girl for her graduation." On a drop cloth in the middle of his living room, was a craftsman-style, four-shelf book case. Two fans blew the pungent scent of varnish out the open windows and patio door.

"It's beautiful." I admired the piece of furniture. "She will be honored. It's a wonderful gift for commencement."

"Hope so." He grinned, pleased with his work. "I'll catch a shower. Be at your place in an hour."

Right on time, Wayne's "rat-a-tat" sounded at the door. I grabbed my black blazer and purse along with directions to the mortuary.

"Let's take my car," I said, and headed out with Wayne following.

After we buckled up, I looked over at him. His gray ponytail was still damp from his shower. His craggy face was clean-shaven. He wore a tan pair of casual pants with a long-sleeved blue shirt, open at the collar. He looked great for the pre-planning ploy, but appeared self-conscious, out of his normal attire of blue jeans and work shirts.

"You look good," I said, sniffing. "Do I smell Old Spice?"

"It is. You've got a good nose," he said, smiling.

"It's great stuff. Thanks for doing this, Wayne." I was grateful he'd gone all out for my plan.

"No problem, kiddo. What are we aiming to get out of this?"

I told him what Jimmy's sister had said about the county giving him a decent burial. I pondered why Jimmy's body had been left in my attic. What had happened between the hospital and the mortuary? Did the hospital have the body, and then it went missing? Was it a mistake? Who knew if we would find anything? I was curious about Mr. Randal.

I filled Wayne in on my cover story for Mr. Randal while I drove. "I'll be Carla, and you be Carl. That way, we won't forget. How about 'Johnson' for a last name? It's a common name, but not like 'Smith.' It sounds more authentic."

"Sure. 'Johnson' works," Wayne agreed.

"How about we call your sick wife, 'Judy'?"

"Judy's good. Got it." Wayne nodded. "I'm Carl Johnson, married to Judy who is dying, and you're the favorite niece, Carla."

"Okay, we're set," I said, satisfied. It sounded simple, easy.

A light drizzle started as we began our trip to the funeral home. The spring rain came in spurts. My wipers cleared the intermittent drops and rubbed against the dry windshield when the showers halted.

I steeled myself, driving on the bumpy black road in front of the mortuary. Water puddled in the holes of the asphalt drive. The funeral home's exterior was a cream-colored stucco. The edges of the black roof had curled, showing signs of age. The driveway was a circular deal, and I parked behind an older black hearse with a dented right front fender.

Memories of the funeral arrangements I had made for Jake, came flooding back. It hadn't been long ago. I forced myself to put them aside. Someday, I'd allow myself the luxury of remembering. Not now. Not today.

Slowly, I emerged from the car, observing the mortuary's setting. The building sat on a deep plot of land. The back of the funeral parlor was bordered by one of the few wooded lots left in the city. The wooded area was overgrown with brush, thick with river birch, red oak, and cottonwood trees.

It appeared as though the lot was being cleared. A burning barrel and narrow limbs from trees were stacked in piles ready to be burned, or taken away beside a path that cut through the forest. A patch of lawn separated the forest from the morgue.

The funeral home's stucco facade was nondescript, the cracked sidewalk led to a double door with glass panels on either side.

Wayne fell into step beside me as we approached the heavy dark doors. The rain began a steady pelt as we proceeded. I held my handbag over my head for an umbrella, and Wayne gingerly pulled the handle of the entry door. It flew open and we were face-to-face with a slightly-built man with deep brown eyes, and thinning, black, greasy hair. I guessed the man to be in his early forties as he greeted us in a worn suit and tie.

"Please, come in," he said. "I'm Jackson Randal, owner and funeral director," and cleared his throat, "How can I help you?"

"We're here to make arrangements for my aunt," I said, momentarily startled by Randal's abrupt appearance.

"Of course; you called earlier," he said, with a slight smile.

"I did."

"Please follow me." We trailed him past a pail, the metal giving a ping as it caught rain drops from the ceiling. He ushered us to a waiting area, and said, "Sorry about the bucket. The roof leaks. Our staff hasn't gotten around to emptying it." He smiled thinly.

"Sure." I glanced at Wayne. He started to smirk; his shoulders trembled as he held back nervous laughter. Mr. Randal's practiced tone smoothly transitioned to, "Tell me about your dear aunt?" His smile was stiff and conciliatory, as if it were practiced and used many times. He looked from Wayne to me.

"Yes. My name is Carla, Carla Johnson. The arrangements are for my Aunt Judy. She's in hospice."

"I'm so sorry," Mr. Randal crooned, and his eyes lit up.

"Part of the problem is, she doesn't have any money left for a big funeral." I was on a roll with my phantom aunt. "The nursing home got all her money." I cleared my throat, adding, "My Uncle Carl, her husband," I nodded at Wayne, "and I are low on funds."

"Retired. Fixed income," Wayne interjected. The light in Mr. Randal's eyes dimmed.

"I'm laid off," I added; it sounded better than unemployed, rehabber, or potential slumlord.

"Huh, huh," Mr. Randal said, his smile stiff. His upper lip stretched across teeth that needed dental work. Brown stains between the teeth reflected oral hygiene neglect, too much tobacco, coffee, or all three.

"Isn't that the way, these days. We see so many people struggling in this economy," he murmured, nodding, clicking his tongue. "We have some very affordable burial plans. We could consider cremation, or view some inexpensive caskets, perhaps," he crooned. "Is your wife an organ donor?" He licked his lips, and smiled.

"No way!" Wayne said. "Don't want my Judy cut up."

"Certainly not," Randal said, his smile faded.

"Oh, I'd like to see the caskets," I exclaimed. Wayne looked ready to run. His expression wary, he was likely wondering if I had gone off the deep end. But, he gulped, shrugging, "Yep, I guess that'd be best."

"Let's go this way." Mr. Randal led us from the reception area through a door off the main lobby. Once inside, I paused and gave a little shudder viewing the line of caskets. Each had a price and description listed below each model. We strolled, surveying the coffins. Wayne turned a shade of gray-green as he ambled along the exhibit. Normally gregarious, and talkative, he was silent. I wondered where the bodies were prepared.

"I need to use a restroom," I said, pivoting towards Mr. Randal.

"Certainly, outside this room is a powder room." He pointed to the door we'd entered, and I made a bee line, leaving Wayne with Mr. Randal to shop for the perfect final resting place for his phantom wife and my imaginary Aunt Judy. I heard Mr. Randal croon to Wayne, "Mr. Johnson, if you would like a few minutes to look, I'll just be in the next room."

Wayne seemed bewildered as Mr. Randal glided through another open door. I glanced through the ajar door as he left. He headed toward a conference room with a long, oblong table and several burgundy-colored, padded chairs.

I winked at Wayne, as I ducked out of the casket display area and rounded the corner. Outside the bathroom, I stopped. There were two doors, one labeled "restroom," the other door, unmarked. I peeked back to the area where I'd left Wayne surveying the coffins. He rubbed his chin as he ambled the length of the coffin display. Mr. Randal was out of sight.

I opened the unmarked door.

It was a walk-in supply closet. I peered at the containers. One shelf held white bottles with black lettering and were labeled *formaldehyde*. The printed labels resembled my latest shampoo. They had a generic appearance with block script against white, similar to containers from the beauty supply store. The other shelves in the closet held paper towels, tissues, toilet paper, all with the same basic labeling. I scanned the shelves.

A loud hacking cough from Wayne alerted me. I stepped from the supply closet, shut the door, and paused outside the restroom, as Mr. Randal came around the corner.

"Are you okay?" Mr. Randal smiled, and asked consolingly. He appeared to materialize out of thin air, standing next to my elbow.

I jumped guiltily. "Yes, just a little weepy." I nodded, grabbing a tissue from my purse, dabbing my nose as if to stop a sniffle. My heart pounded in my chest at nearly being caught snooping.

He searched his pockets and produced a key, saying, "I believe my partner left this door unlocked again." He locked the door and tested the knob. "He can be so forgetful."

"Uh huh." I nodded. I did my best to appear innocent while my shoulders tensed. Sniffling, I left Mr. Randal and joined Wayne in the casket area.

"What home is your wife at?" Mr. Randal asked as he joined us.

"Does it make a difference?' I asked, stalling for time. I hadn't anticipated the question. My blood pressure spiked another fifty points, and I felt my face flush.

"No, no; it shouldn't make any difference as far as her care," Mr. Randal said. Continuing in his silky tone, "With some of the county-run homes we have a financial agreement. The residents are put to rest, shall we say, for a steal?" and gave a light snort.

"They just transferred her to hospice from Colossal Health Hospital," Wayne said, adding, "It's a terrible thing, waiting to die." Looking every bit the anguished husband, he let a few tears flow down his cheeks. His gruff voice caught, and he said, "Just can't think of the name of that danged place." He snuffled and blew his nose vigorously in a white handkerchief he tugged from his back pants pocket.

I viewed Wayne with newfound admiration. If I didn't know better, I would have bought his distraught husband routine, lock, stock, and barrel.

"Of course. I'm sorry, Mr. Johnson," Mr. Randal intoned, and there was no mistaking the interest on his face. "You said Colossal Health? Perhaps I could make inquiries and save you some time and trouble. At times like these, it's understandable your memory may fail," and clucked his tongue.

Wayne let out a howl like a wounded animal and sobbed, burying his head in his handkerchief. I took his arm, "This isn't the best time for my uncle. Could I get your card and we'll try this again another time?" Wayne, in the meantime, had ratcheted up his noisy sobbing with more snorting into his handkerchief.

Mr. Randal pulled a business card from the inside breast pocket of his shabby suit and offered it. "Of course," he said, as I accepted the card. "It is difficult for some men to manage without their wives. It is so refreshing to see a man mourn so freely. It is a testament to the commitment they had." He offered a limp hand. I stuffed his business card into my purse, then took his greasy hand, quickly dropping it.

As Wayne gave another sob, I said, soberly, "Thank you. Yes, yes, they do have quite a relationship." I guided Wayne to the exit. Over my shoulder, I added, "Thank you, Mr. Randal. We'll be in touch."

"There, there, it's okay, Uncle Way … er Carl." I corrected myself and sniffed, smothering a giggle. I kept my arm around Wayne's midsection, acting the comforting niece with her grieving uncle. I felt Mr. Randal's eyes burn holes in the backs of our heads as he watched through the clear glass panels of the funeral home. When we reached the car, I unlocked the passenger's side for Wayne.

"Nice job," I commented, as I came around to the driver's side and buckled in. "You should get an award."

Wayne pressed his handkerchief to his face as though wiping tears of sorrow. His shoulders shook. Tears rolled down his cheeks as he gasped and held his belly, and convulsing into peals of laughter. "Whew, kiddo, you should have seen the look on your face," and he dissolved into more gales of amusement. I snickered. Carried away by the pitch and shaking of Wayne's belly, I sniggered between bursts of laughter.

At home, we sobered up from our meeting with Mr. Randal. We stopped in the hallway outside of Wayne's door at the end of the hall. I sniffed the air as we walked past Mrs. Gilman's unit.

"What do you make of Mr. Randal?" I asked, and added, "besides being creepy." I took another deep whiff outside of Ariel's door, next to Mrs. Gilman's.

"Do you smell that?"

"What?"

"It smells like gasoline and smoke mixed together," I said, considering the odor.

He inhaled deeply. "I see what you mean. My sense of smell isn't what it used to be. I thought Ariel was a health nut." He grinned, and then snorted. "It's not cigarette smoke. It's weed!"

Changing the subject, Wayne went on, "That Randal dude, he's got something going on. A business like that should make enough to fix the roof and have a better hearse," adding, "Kiddo, whenever there's money involved, you have to follow the money."

"Mr. Randal certainly seems slimy enough." The memory of his limp handshake made me cringe. About then, Mrs. Gilman popped out of her unit. She carried a white garbage bag, which was half full. Her expression made me wonder how long she'd been listening at her door.

"Yo, Gillie," Wayne greeted Mrs. Gilman, a wide smile cutting across his face. "How's the new rosebush?"

"Wayne," Mrs. Gilman coyly greeted him, gushing. "It's just beautiful."

She appraised me and said, "Katelyn."

"I gotta go," I said, nodding. "Thanks, Wayne." I retreated to my door. "I'll let you kids catch up," I muttered, as I unlocked my door and let myself in. I doubt they even heard me.

CHAPTER 14

Training at Mega Research Company consisted of thirty minutes with roughly twenty dedicated, market research worker bees, in remote office space at the mall. Jennifer went over the script for the newest products for research—a hemorrhoid cream and diapers. She peppered her presentation with admonitions, "Approach mall shoppers with a smile!"

"The questions are for their benefit," she said. "You are doing them a favor! We are all professionals!" she trilled in a high-pitched voice, impressive with her height, red hair and the passion of a religious zealot. "But, don't linger in front of stores. The owners don't like that! Come back when you've finished two surveys and we'll go from there."

I gritted my teeth and contemplated asking for age and household income, then tactfully inquiring about hemorrhoids. With clipboards in hand, wearing plastic, recycled nametags, all of the trainees were sent to the mall for a test run.

There were rumblings from a few of the people and a couple of twenty-somethings—young men—dropped their materials at the desk on the way out. "This bites," they said, and roared with laughter, slapping each other on the shoulder as they left the pack of newly-minted market surveyors.

I gulped, set my chin, squared my shoulders, and reminded myself this was temporary. "I can do this." I viewed my paperwork and saw the diaper survey. It was a stroke of luck.

I considered my victims—er subjects—as I scrutinized the foot traffic in the mall. I lingered outside the food court, anticipating that people who were full would be more willing to participate. I gave myself a pep talk, trying to convince myself that talking to people would be a welcome diversion from worrying about getting my house sold. Or, trying to solve the mystery of how and why a body had been left in my house.

A smile pasted on my face, I approached two young women with three children between them. One woman had a baby in a carrier facing her chest and midsection. Her baby was sleeping, and she pushed another child in a stroller, who sat up, wide-eyed. The other woman had a toddler, snuggled in a blanket, asleep in another pram. They ambled in tandem, deep in conversation. The woman wearing the papoose-style, baby carrier, idly stroked the child's head as they left an Asian fast-food eatery.

"Excuse me," I approached the young women. "Could I have a few minutes of your time? I'd like to ask a few questions about cloth and disposable diapers." I pointed to the nametag from the research company pinned to my blazer that proved my legitimacy.

"Sure," they said, in unison. "I don't use anything except cloth diapers," one volunteered. "I don't want to gum up our landfills and wreck our planet."

"But you use those plastic underwear pants over the diapers, so they don't leak," the other woman protested. "How is that any better?"

I decided I had the advantage of maturity and a change of topic was in order. "Say, you gals live around here?" Pausing briefly, I asked, "Have you heard anything about bodies left in vacant houses?" I couldn't resist at least one question. Besides, it would be good community outreach to see if they'd heard anything. If word was out about the events, it could affect my home value. Okay, I was obsessed.

"Oh no! That's terrible!" they answered in unison, visibly alarmed.

"Oh, it's probably a rumor," I said quickly. "Sorry. No worries." I smiled to reassure the women.

"Oh, okay," the woman carrying the baby said. "We live here because we want a safe neighborhood for our kids."

"I'm sure it's safe. Probably idle chatter." Silently, I cursed my big mouth. "How about taking my survey so manufacturers can develop an eco-friendly product?" I had seen the word, "eco-friendly," all over and was aching to use it.

With that, the women answered every question and offered opinions on everything diaper-related. When I wrapped up the twenty-minute survey, the woman holding the baby said, "Gee, this was fun! We should do more of these."

"Thank you for your input," I said. I really meant it. News of the bodies hadn't reached the local mainstream, home-buying population. I hoped I hadn't started any gossip.

The other woman piped in, "Are you here often? No one ever asks us what we think about products." She laughed. Startled by the noise, the baby who'd slept through the survey let out a deafening wail. Hurriedly, I let them get on their way.

I was ecstatic that I had finished two surveys and I could take them to the research office for Jennifer, the micro-manager, to review. Even better, neither woman had heard about the bodies. I could market my house, safe in the knowledge that not everyone had heard about the dead body mystery. Maybe, this mess could be solved without a lot of public scrutiny.

Jennifer sat at the front desk doing arm exercises, her long auburn hair pulled back from her face. She paused from flexing her biceps and glanced at her watch as I approached. She beheld me warily, and asked, "Back so soon?"

"I've got the first surveys you wanted?" I formed the statement as a question, thinking from her reaction, I misunderstood the directions.

"Well," she said. "Let's see. Two surveys!"

As she reviewed my responses to the surveys, she beamed and commented, "This is great! I knew you were a market research professional the moment I saw you! Good job!" I felt myself relax, thinking, *yeah, this is what I should be doing. Maybe Jennifer is right; this is my calling.*

"You can finish out tonight and work Friday night. I'll put you on a different survey on Saturday. You're a rock star!" Her excitement was bubbling over.

I felt my life drifting away from me. My feet hurt, but I thought about what I had scheduled for tomorrow and Saturday—nothing, and dead bodies kept popping up in my neighborhood, so I said, "Sure, Jennifer." I could fit in my real job, home-rehab specialist, around consumer research at the mall.

I finished out the night, stopping young mothers and couples with children in tow. Most seemed eager to give any input on diapers and child-rearing. With the exception of a couple of young children who screamed when I approached their parents, I completed what Jennifer called a "record number of surveys." I didn't take the screaming toddlers to heart. After all, there were times I wanted to scream at my appearance too.

I learned my lesson about asking people if they'd heard anything about the dead bodies. If they didn't know, I didn't want to broach the topic.

I poured myself into my car a little after nine o'clock that night. My feet were sore with blisters on the back of each heel. Grateful to be home, I greeted Boots with a pat. He sat on his haunches and watched me with a look of disdain.

"I was out making money, you ungrateful creature."

The cat glared at me and stalked away, his tail in the air. His dish was empty. I kicked off my shoes and went to the cabinet for kitty chow. I grabbed a can of food and stopped, when I caught a whiff of lilacs.

The hair on the back of my neck stood up. I dropped the can and went to the slider. It was open. The scent was from Mrs. Gilman's bushes, next to her patio. My screen was closed. I took a quick glance outside, and threw the door shut, satisfied when it went "clunk." I locked it, took a deep breath, and looked around. The clutter on the kitchen table was the same as when I left.

Boots was interested in the chow on the counter and watched me. I grabbed the tin, opened it and scooped the food into his dish. "I must have forgotten to shut the door," I said, and filled his water bowl.

My nerves still on edge, I grabbed a hammer from the kitchen junk/tool drawer as a weapon and stalked through the townhouse.

The living room and my bedroom were undisturbed. I looked at the stack of boxes in the second bedroom, frowned at the mess and closed the door.

Back in my room, I stashed the hammer in my bedside stand drawer, slipped out of my clothes, put on jammies, washed my face, brushed my teeth, and sank into bed. Sleeping fitfully, I tossed and turned through the night, my mind reliving Jennifer, surveys, and dead bodies; my leg muscles aching.

On the way to the coffeepot the following morning, startled by movement on the sofa, I stopped and shrieked, "Eddy! Eddy, how did you get in here?" I caught my breath as I recognized the shape on my sofa.

Eddy was unfazed by my screams. Grinning with his lazy sleepy, sexy-smoldering attitude, he crooned, "Hey, wifey. You left the patio door open. You can't be doing that. Anybody can just come in. And, you gotta clean out the other bedroom," he added smirking.

I stared at Eddy. He was tall and dark-haired with enough body fat and freckles that added up to movie star handsome. Combined with his easy charm, he could make you feel like you were the most important woman in the universe. It was a combustible combination.

"You hid in the spare bedroom!" Flabbergasted, my voice ratcheted up a full decibel. "I am not your wifey!" I yelled. "You need to leave, now!"

"Easy, take it easy. I fell asleep waiting for you." Eddy grinned, enjoying my anger. Another part and parcel of why we divorced.

In high school, I saw Eddy's laid-back approach to my temper as being positive. He could joke and cajole me out of a sour mood. I learned during the course of our short marriage, his kidding and sweet-talking fueled my anger. My temper gave Eddy a license to go out and do as he might want.

I gave up on Eddy being a faithful mate. I did, however, find him useful on occasion. After Jake died, we developed a mutually beneficial friendship. If I needed someone to move something heavy, I could call on Eddy. He seemed happy with lunch or dinner as payment. I tried not to use his shoulder to cry on, because Eddy, being Eddy, thought it could lead to more.

I wracked my brain trying to recall what favor I'd asked. He gazed at me, sprawled on the sofa, his sparkling brown eyes fringed with long lashes.

"I got lonely," he said. "I miss you."

Suddenly, it clicked. "Lola threw you out," I snapped. "Probably, for the same reasons I kicked you to the curb!"

"You women," Eddy said with mock exasperation, a smile playing on his lips.

"Get out, Eddy," I warned him.

He tossed aside the afghan, weary of the game, and sat up. He wiped the sleep out of his eyes, and ran his hands through sleep-tousled hair, and asked, "Can I have coffee, please?" The years had been kind to Eddy. We were the same age, and he looked the same as the day we married, or the day we divorced.

He had slept in his briefs and tee shirt. He found his faded blue jeans and shirt discarded in a heap on a chair, and dressed. Despite his earlier mockery, he appeared vulnerable. I weakened, feeling a smidge of what we had had early on.

"One cup, and you're out of here," I snapped, steeling myself against a tide of sympathy.

"Thanks." Eddy grinned again. He got up, stretching like a big cat as he went into the bathroom. The sound of the bathroom water traveled through the agape door while I made an extra strong pot of my favorite coffee.

Some time ago, I'd decided after another stretch of austerity, life was too short to drink bad coffee. It was my one luxury.

I opened the blinds and peered out. Mrs. Gilman was on her patio, digging in her flower pots. She wore a floppy gardening hat, cotton gloves, and a hoodie and sweat pants outfit. Her broad-brimmed straw hat sported a blue flower matching the color of her clothing. Large, tortoise shell-colored, sunglasses shaded her eyes, as she filled containers from a flat of flowers on her table.

I waved when she looked towards my window. She began to raise her arm in greeting, then her body stiffened. Behind me, I heard Eddy opening a cupboard door and taking a mug for the fresh java. She pursed her lips and twisted her back to me. With renewed vigor, she potted yellow pansies.

It was eight o'clock in the morning. Mrs. Gilman was offended by the sight of me in pajamas, and likely saw Eddy from her position at the table.

"Believe me, it isn't what you think, Mrs. Gilman."

"Huh?" Eddy asked, grinning. He came up beside me, throwing one arm around my shoulders, while gripping his mug in the other. Giving a sidewise glance, he squeezed me and kissed my forehead.

"Nothing," I said, exasperated, pushing him away. "How about a to-go cup? I have to get to work."

"All right, all right," he protested, while I shoved him towards the door, "I'm going. I'm going."

I showered, threw on my work attire of black blazer, slacks, and a blouse. I did makeup and hair in record time for another shift at the mall, double checking the latch on the patio slider before leaving.

CHAPTER 15

The news about Ariel Kominski's death hit me like a bolt of lightning.

While driving home from my shift at the mall, the local news announced her death on my favorite country western station. The station was playing great songs, "I Love This Bar, " by Toby Keith and a love ballad by Alan Jackson—both terrific tunes. I could laugh at Toby's lyrics and cry at Alan's.

The newscaster broke in saying, "Local woman, Ariel Kominski, heiress to Komin's Grocery stores, dies in tragic bathtub accident. She is thought to be a victim of electrocution. She was found late this afternoon by another resident of the same complex. An investigation is ongoing. More details to follow."

Stunned, I sucked in my breath, and turned the volume up, digesting the news. My brain, numbed by research questions, had a tough time wrapping itself around the idea that Ariel was dead. Could there be another Ariel Kominski? Was it some freakish coincidence of name and location? I doubted it.

At home, I pulled in the parking lot to view a full array of rescue vehicles. The police, fire engine, and ambulance were all in attendance. The emergency vehicles were lined up along the drive and taking their leave. The ambulance left with the sirens eerily silent. Ariel's flashy Jaguar followed the procession, her boyfriend, Paul, was at the wheel. The final vehicle, a white van with blue letters of a news station trailed the Jaguar.

Wayne and Mrs. Gilman watched the convoy from the sidewalk, their faces creased with worry. The lot cleared. I parked, and rushed to the pair.

"I heard about Ariel on the news," and gasping, "What happened?"

"Found her in the tub. Dead as a doornail. Don't know why they sent an ambulance," Wayne muttered, staring at the pavement, "She was already dead."

"I'm sure it's SOP," I said, my breath calming and logic taking over.

"Huh?" Wayne asked.

"Standard operating procedure," I offered. "They have to do an autopsy to determine the cause of death."

"There was a hairdryer in the tub. No need to do an autopsy. Waste of money, I tell you," Wayne grumbled. "Told the cops that, too. They called the coroner. He said she was dead, like I said," he snorted. "He didn't like the looks of it, so they had detectives sniffing around."

Wayne looked like he needed a stiff drink. He took out a pack of Camel's unfiltered cigarettes from the front pocket of his work shirt and tapped one out, lit up, and took a deep drag. Mrs. Gilman and I discretely avoided the path of the smoke.

"How do you know?" I asked, puzzled.

"Her door was open." Wayne paused between deep pulls on his cigarette, his voice low and rough, as he inhaled. "She asked me to build a shelf. Finished it. Thought I'd drop it off. Her door was ajar. I knocked, opened the door, and yelled, 'Ariel.' Got no answer. Was going to leave the shelf inside. Heard running water, sounded like it was coming from the bathroom. Living room carpet was soaked—so I took a gander."

His hand trembled as he took a drag from his cigarette and went on, "She was face up in the tub wearing a robe, water spigots on full blast, hairdryer in the tub. I unplugged the hairdryer, cranked off the faucets, ran, and called 9-1-1."

"The news said she was electrocuted," I said, watching Wayne's face.

"Yeah, looked like she slipped and fell, and took the dryer with her." Wayne took another deep puff from his cigarette.

"Seems curious to be drying your hair when you're running tub water," I pondered aloud.

"Looked like she was getting ready for a guest," he offered, flicking ash from his cigarette.

"What do you mean?" Mrs. Gilman asked.

"All kinds of fancy candles laid out. Bottle of champagne chilling in the sink. Ariel's robe wasn't any I'd ever seen a woman wear for a bath. It was a real fancy, silky kind of thing."

"Oh!" Mrs. Gilman exclaimed.

"So, she was preparing to entertain, and celebrate with a special someone. Her beau, Paul?" I asked.

"I guess. Like I told the cops, I didn't see nobody." Wayne reached the end of his cigarette and tossed it to the ground, putting it out with the heel of his shoe. He picked up the butt and field-stripped it, scattering the rest of the tobacco.

"Her boyfriend came the same time as the police and ambulance," Mrs. Gilman said.

"He was driving her fancy car, squealing the tires. Such reckless driving," she added, shaking her head in distain.

"Did he know something was wrong? Maybe that was why he was in a hurry?" I asked.

"Maybe." Mrs. Gilman appeared disappointed. "I suppose it might account for his driving."

"You know, if I was a betting man," Wayne said, "I'd figure the likes of him would have done her in."

"Why do you say that?" I asked.

"Just a hunch. He looks creepy, slimy. And he shows up with the police. Seems mighty strange," Wayne said, and shrugged, "like he was waiting, or something."

"Huh?" I shook my head. I agreed with Wayne about Ariel's suitor. But it wasn't for me to offer opinions on the creepiness of someone else's love interest. I had my own demons to consider, when I thought about the toads I'd kissed before I'd met and married Jake.

"Creepy or slimy doesn't mean he's a murderer," I ventured.

"It sure don't hurt none," he said, and guffawed.

"True enough," I agreed. "Are the police coming back?"

"Don't look like it," Wayne said. "No, don't think so. No yellow tape anyway."

"Ariel's boyfriend locked up the place. I overheard one of the detectives say, 'Looks like an accident,' as they left," Mrs. Gilman offered.

"So, Ariel's boyfriend has a key to her unit?" I asked.

"That is correct, Katelyn Baxter." Wayne's smirk and the use of my full name caught my attention.

"But," I said, lifting my eyebrows, watching Wayne, "that doesn't mean someone couldn't enter the premises?"

"That is also correct, kiddo," Wayne said, eyes twinkling with anticipation.

"Well, what are we waiting for?" Mrs. Gilman piped up. "Let's get on with it."

I marveled that Mrs. Gilman was turning out to be quite the spy, as we trooped down the hall to Ariel's door. We waited while Wayne, with astonishing speed, took a tool from his jeans pocket and jimmied the lock. He threw open the door. Silence greeted us from the dark entry of the townhome.

"I'll stay here and be a lookout," Mrs. Gilman whispered. Her face had a white pallor in the dimly lit hallway.

"You're the best, Gillie," Wayne returned. Mrs. Gilman beamed at his compliment. "Use the code word, 'redrum,' if anyone comes," he added.

"Redrum," Mrs. Gilman repeated, nodding, her face glowing with Wayne's attention.

I studied Wayne. "Redrum?"

He winked and shrugged. "What?" he asked, "It's from *The Shining*, with Jack Nicholson, one of the greatest movies ever made. It's "murder" spelled backwards."

"Oh."

"You should see it. It's a great movie."

"I have seen it," I said, adding, "Just didn't come to mind right now." My nerves were frayed from breaking and entering Ariel's house. I shook my head in disbelief that Wayne could jest at a time like this, but he did have a dark sense of humor.

Wayne flipped the wall switch and took the lead, waving me in behind him.

I followed on tiptoe, my shoes squishing through the soaked hall carpet to the bath adjoining the master bedroom. Unconsciously, I held my breath as we made our way through Ariel's bedroom.

I tried not to stare at the bedroom walls, taking a left into the bathroom. My brief glimpse of the room made me think *bordello*. It was painted a deep purple. The window treatments were a floor length, satin, with a filmy ecru colored swag, adorned with glass jewelry-like fringe. Not my taste, but each to their own. The bedding was in disarray, as if it had been searched—the pillows taken out of shams, along with an assortment of throw pillows scattered about.

Wayne saw my expression and suggested, "Maybe she was making up the bed?"

"Maybe," I muttered. The bathroom color matched the bedroom. There were two purple shag throw rugs and a light beige shower curtain.

True to Wayne's account, one corner of the tub held a thick round candle within a glass cylinder, another corner held smaller votive candles. The large candle gave off a sweet vanilla scent. None had been lit. One long-stemmed, red rose in a crystal vase adorned the toilet tank. A compact disc player, loaded with a CD was on one side of the vase. The CD's plastic cover, titled *Sax on the Beach* was propped against the wall. Perfect music for a romantic rendezvous. Too bad the evening had proved fatal for Ariel.

The tub was drained. Towels littered the floor, absorbing the overflow of water. The corner of the tub closest to the faucet held a white bottle that looked like shampoo. The housing for the dryer was on one side of the mirror. An over-the-tank shelf held every kind of bath salts, cream, and toiletry product. A pair of crystal champagne flutes were tucked into the unit next to bubble bath.

"Doesn't look like code," I said, pointing at the dryer compartment.

"No, sure don't," he agreed. "Outlet's too close to the tub."

"What do you suppose the occasion was?" I asked, stooping to get a better view of the bottle of champagne in the sink. The sink held water with traces of melting ice.

"Don't know a lot about Ariel. Could be rich kids buy this stuff for any time. It's not as special to them as it would be to us working stiffs. Good God, how much you suppose a bottle of this goes for these days?" Standing next to me, he leaned over and peered at the bottle's label. "This here says it's DomDom Perignon. It's fake. It's fake champagne!" Wayne let loose a huge belly laugh, and the sound broke the tension.

"Maybe Ariel didn't have as much money as she wanted people to believe she had?" I speculated.

"Redrum! Redrum!" we heard Mrs. Gilman warble outside Ariel's door.

"You go first. I'll lock up," Wayne urged. "Hurry!"

I dashed from the bathroom, through the master bedroom, and out to the central corridor. I met up with Mrs. Gilman where she had stalled Ariel's boyfriend. She blocked Paul's view, standing with one hand on the wall, the other on her hip, as she diverted his attention from Ariel's door.

"Simply dreadful. Tsk, tsk," I heard her cluck to Paul.

He was subdued and sullen. There was the hint of a smile on his petulant face, which appeared unwarranted for the events.

"Seems like an overwrought lover would shed a few tears," I muttered under my breath.

Keeping the boyfriend at bay and oblivious was the order of the moment while Wayne was away from our little group. I stood shoulder to shoulder beside Mrs. Gilman, and together we blocked the hallway.

"Sorry to hear about Ariel," I offered. I was sorry. Just not terribly sorry, when I recalled the times, she had critiqued my food choices and bragged about her wealth.

Wayne joined us a moment later. "Bummer," he said, offering his hand to Paul. "If you need anything, just give a knock."

Paul ignored Wayne's gesture, and wasn't moved by our collective expressions of sympathy. "Thanks, I'd better be going," he nodded, edging around us, and headed to Ariel's door. His hair looked as if he'd added an extra layer of grease to keep it in place.

"Oh, are you staying in Ariel's place tonight?" Mrs. Gilman asked, doubt clouding her face, and asked, "Is that a good idea?"

"Uh, no. I'm staying at my mother's. I forgot something." It sounded like a feeble excuse to get back into the townhouse. Ironic, since we'd just done a break and enter. The three of us nodded and murmured in unison as we watched Paul unlock the door to Ariel's house.

"Seems odd," I said, after he shut the door behind him.

"Which part? The part about staying with his mother, or the part about forgetting something?" Wayne grunted, and said in a low voice, "If you ask me, the dude smells of odd."

"I absolutely agree, Wayne," Mrs. Gilman said. "He didn't seem very upset about Ariel. Shouldn't he be with her? I'd hope my Walter would have shown a little more emotion if he'd learned I was found dead in the bathtub," she declared.

"They say everyone grieves differently," I said. "But what could be so important that Paul would leave Ariel's side and come back to an empty house to retrieve something? What could he get here that his mother wouldn't have at her place?"

"He's up to no good," Wayne said. "I know it."

"Oh, Wayne, you're so smart." Mrs. Gilman looked up at the lanky handyman, smiling.

I felt like a third wheel watching the seniors exchange adoring smiles. After an awkward silence, I said, "I'm sure our sheriff will be able to get to the bottom of this.

I'll just say goodnight." I backed away from the lovebirds.

I unlocked and opened the door to my home. Mrs. Gilman and Wayne disappeared into Mrs. Gilman's townhome. I was halfway inside and hesitated, when I saw Paul leaving Ariel's unit, carrying a brown paper bag. I closed my door, pondering what could be in the package.

"Yowl! Yowl! Yowl!" Boots leaped from the corner near his food bowl, pouncing at my legs.

"All right, already!" I got Boots' chow and filled his water bowl. He gulped his dinner. Calmer, the dish empty, he stalked to the sofa, hopped up, and cleaned his face. It felt good to be needed.

I tucked myself into bed, where the image of Paul leaving Ariel's unit, mingled with Wayne's amazing ability to break and enter, lulled me into a troubled sleep.

CHAPTER 16

Worn out by the events of the previous night, I dragged myself to the mall for surveys the next day. Boots needed chow. I needed chow. I put Ariel's death in the back of my mind while I made money.

"We need men between the ages of forty and seventy with hemorrhoids, who want to give input on treatments they use. Work smart, not hard," Jennifer warned, her intensity fairly seeping from her pores. "Focus on the proper age and gender demographic. I know you can do it!" She smiled, shoving a clipboard in my hands. The dreaded hemorrhoid studies. I'd done so well on the diaper survey; it was a no-brainer for Jennifer to challenge my skill set.

I tried to look professional when I approached a man with gray hair who appeared to be the right age group for the survey.

"You gotta be kidding," the man exclaimed, as I explained the survey. "You people are like vultures in this mall; I gotta get a birthday gift for my wife or she's gonna kill me."

I yelled, "Thank you," after him as he ran off. He twisted and scowled as he made a beeline towards a department store.

The next man was with a woman I guessed was his wife. Perhaps, it would be less creepy if I asked a couple.

The woman answered for the gentlemen, "Oh, Bertie doesn't want to answer any questions about hemorrhoids. He wouldn't say if he had them. Which he DOESN'T," she emphasized, "do you, Bertie?"

Bertie grimaced, and shook his head "no." They hurried off.

The night dragged on, and I was showing zilch for completed surveys. Jennifer would not be pleased. I retreated to a corner of the mall next to an electronics store. I wanted to study the crowd for my next victim, as I was beginning to think of those unfortunate enough to be singled out by market researchers.

While I collected myself, the prospect of Ariel's death and the unsolved mystery of why bodies were being randomly left in empty houses crept into my thoughts. Wayne's eagerness to get inside Ariel's apartment hadn't gone unnoticed. Uneasily, I considered how he might have known about the body left in the attic of the Bluebird Street house, and his presence at Ariel's house the night of her death. Myra said she had called him, which is why he knew about the "stiff," as he referred to Jimmy Woo. But, had he been a little too eager to get into Ariel's house after her death?

A man jostled me as he passed, interrupting my thoughts. "Excuse me," he said absently. About to leave the store, he closed his shopping bag and put his wallet in his back pants pocket.

"No problem," I answered, my earlier thoughts vanished, and I reviewed the survey questions, considering how to ask them in the best possible light.

"Ahem," the man cleared his throat.

I glanced up from the form and into the deep blue eyes of Sheriff Don Williams.

Staring, my stomach flipped as he held my gaze. He broke our eye lock by observing my clipboard and temp tag. "You're working for the research company?"

My snappy black blazer and slacks felt frumpy under his watchful eyes. I cursed my wild hair and knew my lipstick had worn off. Bit away, as man after man rejected participation in my study, not to mention my guilty thoughts about Wayne.

"Yes, I am. Until my house is sold," I said, adding, "I like talking to new people and getting feedback on products, *I should cross my fingers to cancel out that whopper of a lie.* I gripped my clipboard in both hands as my palms started to sweat.

"Uh huh." He sounded skeptical, and I pressed my lips together, and bit my bottom lip to stop any brighter commentary. He smiled at me, the lines at his eyes crinkling.

"What's the matter? You don't want me to answer your survey?" he asked in a low voice. He observed my arms clutching the questionnaire against my chest, and lightly patted my shoulder. I tensed.

"Uh, don't think you're quite right for it." I hugged the clipboard to my chest, avoiding his gaze, cursing the blush I felt warming my face. His touch had set off a spark of electricity warming the area, the heat traveling down my arm. My face was on fire. "Anything new on the investigation, Sheriff?" I blurted. Meanwhile, *I wouldn't be doing this job, if the work on my house hadn't been delayed by a slow police investigation.* But I bit my tongue.

"Nothing new. We'll be in touch, Katelyn."

Mentally, I kicked myself. I felt like a giddy school girl. He remembered my name.

"Just don't block the entrances. You might get run over," he admonished. He strode off, treating me to another view of his broad shoulders.

"Hey, you ran into me …" I countered, but he was gone. It was just as well. It sounded argumentative. Not a good tone to take with an officer of the law. The stomach flip I felt from our accidental encounter went to a deep flop.

I was sure he was clueless about any attraction I felt, and decided to give up the fantasy. I went back to the job at hand. My run-in with Sheriff Don set the tone for the rest of the night. Male after male I approached ignored me, avoided, or ran after my opening statement. Time was running out. I panicked. With panic, came aggression.

In a final act of desperation, I stopped a kindly looking gentleman with silver hair and a craggy, age-lined face. He wore dark brown, thick, plastic-rimmed eyeglass frames.

"What?" he asked, puzzled, and frowning, while fiddling with his hearing aid.

"I have a survey," I yelled.

"What?" The man stared at me, his face contorted, trying to read my lips.

"A survey! Research!"

"I can't hear you!" He was becoming more agitated, cocking his head, and shrugging his shoulders in irritation. I pointed to the first paragraph on the survey. His eyes got large and angry as he read the subject of the research. He grimaced with the look of dismay I'd seen from all the men I'd queried.

"Harrumph," he said, and stomped off, still adjusting his hearing aid.

I considered filling in a few surveys to make my statistics appear better.

Or, make it appear as though I had done any studies, at all. Then, I rejected that possibility. I didn't know the ramifications of bogus research, but I was darned if I would be the source of dishonest study material. I had my honor after all. Unfortunately, integrity doesn't pay the bills.

I marched back to the consumer research office to face Jennifer. And, practically jumped for joy when I learned she'd left for the day. The woman who took my papers, nodded an acknowledgement. If she saw none were filled in, she didn't comment, or didn't care. It had been a dismal day for consumer research.

I left in a funk. My accidental meeting with the sheriff had left me depressed. I wasn't any closer to discovering who'd left the bodies in the neighborhood. I was tanking as a consumer researcher. Now, Ariel's death complicated matters and my suspicions about Wayne nagged at me. I got into my car, my mind on overload. It was fortunate the car knew the way home.

I let myself in. Lights shimmered from Mrs. Gilman's patio, reflecting in the kitchen between the vertical blinds. I went to the slider, drew aside the window covering and looked out. Mrs. Gilman and Wayne were seated at her outdoor table kibitzing. Wayne saw me and motioned me to join them. My stomach gave a dull thud. I mouthed, "in a minute." I fed Boots, who was still sulking after last night's neglect. He gave me a reproachful look, and gobbled his chow. I scarfed down a cold piece of pizza, standing at the sink, thinking of my doubts about Wayne.

Grabbing a light beer from the refrigerator, I went out and joined them.

"What's up?" I asked, settling in the cushions of the black wrought iron chairs.

"The police were out asking questions today," Mrs. Gilman said, with a worried expression. "They said Ariel's death wasn't an accident like they first thought. They think   someone threw the hairdryer in the tub. She didn't lose her balance and fall." She paused, looking at Wayne.

"The cops think she was shoved in the tub," he said.

"Oh my," I said, taken aback at the mental image of Ariel flailing while a hair dryer was tossed in the tub. "Who could have hated Ariel so much they would resort to electrocution?" I asked, shuddering.

"The police don't know. They're still investigating," Mrs. Gilman said, adding, "The men took apart the tub drain." Leaning towards me, in a hushed tone, she added, "I heard them say the medical examiner found bruises around Ariel's neck, like someone strangled her. Mind you, I was gardening. I wasn't eavesdropping," she insisted. "They didn't keep their voices down or anything. It was like they were talking about the weather."

"What were they looking for?"

"Well, they bagged up something in one of their little kits before they left," Mrs. Gilman said, her brows furrowed, lips pursed.

"Did you hear what they found, Gillie?" Wayne asked, his voice low.

I strained to hear, all nerves on edge.

"I think it was a chain or something," Mrs. Gilman whispered.

"Her necklace!" Wayne and I said together. We had seen Ariel wearing the cross prominently presented on a silver chain.

"Shush," Mrs. Gilman whispered looking around. "Yes. I think that was it."

"It was found in the drain trap?" I asked. "That means, the water spigot was off."

"Dang it, kiddo. You're right!" Wayne exclaimed. I relaxed when he used my nickname, adding, "The killer must have strangled her using the necklace. In the scuffle, it broke, and he grabbed the cross, the chain slipped off and slid into the drain. The culprit was so distraught; he did the first thing that came to mind."

"Which was to shut the drain, start the bath water, and pitch the dryer into the tub. Fool everyone into thinking it was an accident," Wayne finished with a flourish, reaching for his smokes.

"He staged the bathroom scene!" Mrs. Gilman exclaimed.

"Bingo," I said, raising my beer and nodding.

"My, who would have thought anyone would try to disguise a homicide?" Mrs. Gilman said, shaking her head.

"The marks on her neck would make it murder," I said, taking a sip.

"The cops are looking at everyone in Ariel's life as a possible murderer," Wayne grumped. "Never did like that woman, Ariel. Troublemaker. Through and through," he snorted. "Yep, it's murder, all right. I bet they find plenty from that necklace," then adding, "I touched the danged champagne bottle and the faucet handles. My prints are on the shelf I left in the entry. Dom Dom Perignon, indeed!"

"We were both in Ariel's bathroom after she died," I said, giving Wayne the benefit of the doubt. I searched my memory of the scene. Had I touched something by accident? I didn't think I had, given my recent troubles with Jimmy Woo's body in my rehabbed house. The sheriff's warning at the scene, 'not to touch anything' had been burned into my brain.

"It seems logical, Ariel's townhouse was contaminated, because it was never taped off," I said, and queried, "Besides, what possible motive would any of us have to kill her?"

In the dim light of the patio, Mrs. Gilman's expression was glum. Wayne's attitude matched.

"Well, Ariel wasn't the most pleasant," she said, "I don't want to speak ill of the dead, but she always made little remarks about how it would be healthier if I grew vegetables and herbs, instead of flowers, in my pots. It was a better use of nature's resources to grow food, she would say." Mrs. Gilman sniffed, and brushed a leaf from her pants.

"Your flowers are beautiful! I can't think of doing anything better with Mother Nature, then making our surroundings beautiful with flowers!" Wayne's voice thundered.

"I agree, Mrs. Gilman."

"Thank you," she said, beaming at our approval. "It's just, Ariel gave the impression she looked down at my flowers, and my clothing for gardening." She was wearing another of her 'outfits'—a fuchsia-colored hoodie and sweat pants. "She never came out and said anything. It was the way she looked at me." Shaking her head, she added, "I could be wrong."

I didn't doubt Mrs. Gilman's interpretation of Ariel's demeanor. I was familiar with the dismissive glances she'd leveled my way. She could be tacky and snooty at the same time.

"Gillie, you look hot to me," Wayne said, chuckling.

Mrs. Gilman blushed, and I rolled my eyes. It was embarrassing how smitten they were with each other. But I'm easily embarrassed at people's public displays of affection.

I recalled Ariel's disdain when she once saw an empty pizza carton of mine and said, "If that's a motive for murder, then I'm a suspect too. Ariel didn't approve of my food choices. Thank goodness I don't have any planters out."

"Lord knows, how she tolerated my cigarettes. I know what she thought of AA though," he grumbled. We watched Wayne, waiting for his explanation. "She said I was weak going to AA meetings. She said anyone could overcome an addiction by sheer willpower," and grunted, "Then, she stiffed me for the price of the first shelf. Said, it didn't meet her standards, and could I please do another?"

Mrs. Gilman and I looked at each other in amazement. Wayne's skill as a carpenter was top notch, as far as we were concerned.

"Heck, I'd kill her myself, if she wasn't already dead," Wayne declared.

"You don't mean that," I said. My earlier doubts about Wayne evaporated. Anyone who suggested he would kill someone if they weren't already dead, was probably innocent. If he'd really killed her, he'd likely be quiet.

"Wayne, no!" Mrs. Gilman said, searching his expression.

"Well, no. But I sure don't miss her. That's a fact!"

Mrs. Gilman and I kept quiet. I agreed with Wayne and thought Mrs. Gilman did, too. But, to say it out loud didn't seem very charitable at the moment. Especially, since there appeared to be a murderer afoot.

"My money is on the boyfriend. He's just plain scary," Wayne declared.

"They say in most cases, it's the spouse, close friend, or relative to the deceased who will do them in," Mrs. Gilman agreed, adding, "Emotions run amok." She let out a breath and ran her fingers through her hair.

"That's true," I said, and nodded. "What do we know about her boyfriend, Paul?"

"Danged if I know a lot about him." Wayne shrugged his shoulders. "He showed up one morning and Ariel was wrapped around him like a cheap suit."

Mrs. Gilman smiled, lowered her eyes, and said in a small voice, "I know Ariel and Paul had their lovers' spats."

Wayne and I looked at Mrs. Gilman, surprised.

"I can't help but hear what goes on in anyone's unit, with windows and doors open, you know," she said, embarrassed. "It's not like I'm snooping or anything. These walls are pretty thin."

A brief picture of Mrs. Gilman, her ear pressed to the adjoining wall of our townhomes, flashed through my mind. I resolved to beef up the insulation in my unit to block any random sounds coming from my home. It would help with the heating and cooling budget, too.

"What did they fight about?" I quizzed Mrs. Gilman.

"Well, there was one time," she reflected aloud, pursing her lips, "I heard him ask Ariel why he should pay all the bills, when her family had all the money?" Her voice rose, recounting the memory and she insisted, "He was quite angry. I believe he even swore, calling her vulgar names."

"What did she say? Could you hear?" I asked.

"Well," Mrs. Gilman said, deliberately, "she told him there wasn't any more family money. She was out of the will. The most he would get from being with her was her prominent family connections. If that wasn't enough, he could get out."

"Did he leave?" I asked.

"Well, the door slammed so hard I thought my pictures were going to come off the wall," she admitted. "But he was back later in the day and they were all hot and heavy by noon. "There was a funny smell coming from the house," she said, and she wrinkled her nose.

"Smell? What kind of smell?" I asked, watching her.

"I'm not sure. Not cigarettes. Not plain old cigarettes," she recalled, then shrugging her shoulders. "My guess is it was marijuana."

"I knew there was something funny with those two," Wayne slapped his knee. "Health nut, phooey! It was something stronger than marijuana!"

"What do you mean?" I asked, my head tilted, quizzical.

"Back in the day," he said, "it was the rage when I was getting clean, they were starting to smoke wacky weed, wet," and he winked.

"Good heavens. What does that mean?" Mrs. Gilman exclaimed, and paused, breathless, waiting for Wayne to explain.

"Potheads would soak marijuana in embalming fluid. It gave the weed an extra kick. Mind you, I never did," he went on. "As far as I could see—it was a waste of a joint. Some guys tripped out and hallucinated on the stuff. It didn't make you feel high, just out of it. A person didn't know what they were doing, seeing, or hearing."

"Is that right?" Mrs. Gilman asked, incredulous.

"Yep."

"The odd smell could have been a mixture of marijuana and embalming fluid or formaldehyde?" I asked.

"Gillie, you sure it didn't smell like gasoline burning, not a joint being smoked?"

"That's it! That's what I smelled!"

"That could explain the loud arguments. If someone is seeing or hearing things that aren't there … maybe both people are hallucinating, it could lead to some loud discussions," I elaborated.

"You betcha it could," Wayne said, snorting, slapping his knee.

"I remember that day," I said, thinking back. "I was job hunting that morning and my patio door was shut. I didn't hear the fight. I heard the make-up part when I opened the door over lunch," I went on, recalling the ecstasy of cooing voices.

"I must have been working in the garage or at the house on Bluebird. I missed the fight and the 'hot and heavy' part," Wayne said, chuckling. "I'm right next door. I would have heard everything."

"Who paid for the fancy car?" I wondered aloud.

"Oh, she did," Mrs. Gilman said. "It was a leased car, that was part of the fight. 'Cost a fortune to ride around like a f'ing… diva!' Paul yelled." She flushed bright red at the expletive, and added, "she said he didn't have to worry about the car—the dealer was about to take it back. She hadn't made the payments for months."

"She wasn't making her car payments. What about the townhouse payments? Was there a mortgage?" I asked, studying Mrs. Gilman as she shifted on her chair.

"She was going to lose her house," Mrs. Gilman said, uncomfortable, reaching for her drink, "Now, it takes longer for the bank to take a house back with all the foreclosures around."

"That's why she bought fake champagne," Wayne said, and guffawed.

"Indeed. What were they celebrating? Presuming, the evening was a happy occasion for them?" I asked. "If Ariel wasn't spending her money on her bills, what was she spending it on?"

"Who knows, with that pair?" Wayne exclaimed. "I bet she would have stiffed me for the second shelf!"

I agreed with Wayne. My earlier reservations about Wayne were put to rest; he would have gladly given Ariel the shelf, if she'd had the guts to tell him she didn't have the money.

Hesitating, Mrs. Gilman offered, "Well, she got a lot of deliveries from UPS. I think she might have spent too much shopping online. Just a thought."

"Great. Just great. That tears it for me," Wayne said, grumbling. "I'm going in. I'll say good-night. Ladies." He nodded, and got up from the table.

"Good night, Wayne," Mrs. Gilman said. He stooped to give her a peck on her cheek, and said, "Good night, Gillie," making her blush. He threw out a "'night, kiddo," to me and headed to his townhouse.

I yawned, rising after he left. "I'll be off. Good night, and thanks, Mrs. Gilman, for your hospitality and information."

I was half way through my patio slider as she got up and started towards her unit, saying "Good evening, Katelyn."

"'Night, Mrs. Gilman," I repeated, shutting the slider behind me. *I have to get this house better insulated.*

CHAPTER 17

News of Ariel's death reached a fevered pitch on local broadcasts. Her death was labeled a homicide. Instead of "Local Woman Dies in Tragic Bathtub Accident," the headlines ballooned to "Local Heiress to Komin's Grocery Empire Dies in Deadly Bathtub Strangulation: A Murderer Is on the Lam!" Local stations gave "breaking news" updates throughout the day.

Ironically as it turned out, the name "Kominski" was the only real thing about Ariel. Her ancestors had changed the name of their store to a shortened version of their surname. Ariel had come from money and was in line to inherit a major portion of the grocery empire. She hadn't been honest with Paul. Ariel had family connections, and family money.

I wondered how the will sat with Paul, now that Ariel was gone. Did she lie because more than one suitor considered her to be a meal ticket, rather than a soul mate?

Investigating the dead bodies in vacant houses stalled with Ariel's murder. I didn't think there was any reason for the sheriff to consider me a suspect in her death. I had a little resentment over her claims to superior food choices, but that was it. Pretty slim motive for murder. That's what I told myself. Besides, I was at work when it happened.

The people or person behind the bodies in the foreclosed houses must have an inside track on which houses were vacant, I reasoned. And, they must have known they wouldn't arouse suspicion. Wondering if another random body would show up in my neighborhood was taking its toll. So was worry about my finances as I grabbed whatever shifts Jennifer threw my way. It was prudent to add another stream of income.

My interview for wine tasting hostess was scheduled for nine o'clock in the morning. I entered the office of the wine and beer distributor and met with two women. One was a brunette, Roxy; the other was a blonde named Meg. They appeared to be in their mid-forties and were in good humor.

"Thank goodness; she looks normal," Roxy said, after introductions. Chuckling, she glanced at Meg.

"She'll do well," Meg said, agreeably.

Roxy added, "You wouldn't believe the different people we get applying for this job."

"I'll bet."

"Why do you want to give out wine samples?" Meg asked.

"I enjoy wine, and it's an opportunity to make extra money," I said, adding, "I'm a Home Renovation Specialist. Renovations are taking longer than anticipated. The market is soft right now."

"Ah," Roxy said. She nodded, adding, "The state of the economy."

"The good thing about the economic downturn is," Meg chimed in, "people are drinking more. Our business is booming, which is why we're adding staff. We have a new merlot we're promoting for spring and summer."

"I love wine. All kinds." I preferred white, but they didn't need to know my favorite. It was an interview; people always stretched the truth.

"We have a couple of stores with tastings set for this week. Wear a white top, black slacks, and bring a bottle opener and a tray to put the samples on," Roxy said, and then asked, "Your license and social security card?"

"Here." I offered my identification cards to Roxy, who gave them to Meg, who made copies. Roxy handed the documentation back, saying, "Stock will be at the store. Just take what you need for the tasting. A table cloth is always nice. Any questions?"

"When and where?"

She wrote the name of the store and particulars on a piece of paper and handed it to me, "You can start tomorrow."

"Great." I walked out feeling like I'd won the lottery. Easy peasy. This was going to be a great little gig.

I picked up a few groceries on the way home. More coffee, peanut butter, and frozen pizza for me. Kitty food for Boots. I stopped to pick up the mail. Along with a stack of bills was my perpetual Publisher's Clearing House envelope. For people uninformed about this outfit, when you subscribe to magazines, you have the 'opportunity' to enter their contests. I haven't purchased magazines for years, but I'm still on the mailing list.

I don't gamble. Gambling is like throwing money down a rat hole. I do, however, send each and every one of my entry cards to PCH. For twenty years, I have waited for the prize patrol and Dave Sayer, their pitchman, to drive to my house and deliver my winnings. It's my little dream.

I gave Boots a treat from a jar on the counter which he grabbed and scampered off with. I finished putting away my provisions. I felt lucky after my interview with Roxy and Meg. It could be a sign, finally, that good fortune could be mine. I ripped open the mailer from PCH, slapped the stickers in the appropriate spaces on the return card, stamped it, and trekked it to the postal box.

Back inside, I opened the slider to air out my tiny kitchen. Mrs. Gilman was fussing with her petunias and geraniums. We exchanged a brief smile and a nod.

The townhouse complex was quiet in the aftermath of Ariel's death. Crime scene tape was stretched across the front of her door. It was too little, too late, given that Wayne and I were able to get into her house. Not to mention, Ariel's boyfriend had gone in and out at will. Now, I knew Ariel's house would be foreclosed on, and I considered whether there could be an investment opportunity for me there. I nixed the idea.

It was one thing when a body was left in a vacant home. It was totally different when someone died a tragic death while living in the house. Terrible karma. Lord knows, I didn't need nasty vibes. Something nagged at me about the bathroom. I couldn't quite put my finger on it.

I headed to my bedroom to take a short nap before my stint at the mall.

I woke with a start and looked at my watch. "Dang it!" Boots was curled up on the pillow next to mine.

"You were supposed to wake me!" I glared at the cat. I made a dash for the bathroom, threw on makeup, and ran a brush through my hair.

I sprayed my hair into submission. As I styled it, I spotted my shampoo bottle in the bath bay. I stopped in mid-spray. The scene from Ariel's bathroom came to mind.

Eureka! I knew what Paul was after. Breathless, I slipped into my standard uniform for mall research and pretty much any other occasion.

I put the news about Ariel's death in the back of my mind as I ventured out to the mall for the night's surveys. My mind and body were on autopilot as I stopped shoppers in mid-stride and asked women about cooking oils. Work smart, not hard—Jennifer's admonition to the surveyors, echoed in my mind as I eyed patrons.

It was smarter to ask women over men about using olive oil as opposed canola oil in the kitchen. A question lost on someone like myself, whose culinary skills are limited.

Ruefully, this would be a good survey to talk to Myra about. She had the interest and talent for gourmet cooking. I considered padding my total surveys with a call to Myra. I thought better of it when I considered Jennifer's temperament. I was never one to challenge authority. Better to duck, or run from it.

I was in desperate need of a sounding board for the events of the past couple days. My lifeline, Myra, had been silent. I wondered if she'd heard about Ariel on the news, and thought I would bring her up to speed by calling during my break.

"Oh, hi—can I call you back? I've got the security camera people here right now." Myra sounded out of breath.

"Security camera?"

"Yes. I've had quite enough. They got away with another wreath from my door," Myra said, sounding exasperated. She decorates with several wreaths. One every season: spring, summer, fall, winter and one for Christmas. Once in a while, she'll have a dual-purpose wreath. One year, a winter-themed wreath stayed up through Christmas and another year she had a spring-summer wreath. They are quite elaborate and she spends plenty to decorate her front door.

The disappearing decorations had been an ongoing situation which never warranted a lot of comment. She suspected it was neighborhood kids out for a cheap thrill. She tried motion-activated lights but gave up on those when the occasional jay-walking goose or rabbit set them off. The flash of lights annoyed her when they reflected into her bedroom. By the time she got to the front door, the wreath was inevitably gone. And, she reasoned, what could she do if she confronted the thief?

Lately, she had dealt with the pilfering by tying the wreath to the hook, which she deemed as tacky. It proved to be the best solution until the culprit brought something to cut the floral tape holding the wreath to the hook. She started using a heavy gauge green wire to blend and hold the wreath more firmly.

"They must have wire cutters," Myra said. "I am darn well going to find out who is doing this. This is not acceptable. I am installing a security camera that will focus on the door. I'll take the film to my brother to deal with this."

"How much does a security system cost?"

"You don't want to know. Besides, it's the principle of the matter. It's an invasion of privacy and theft. If they have a wire cutter, it could be a deadly weapon," she said, her words clipped in a no-nonsense tone.

"Of course," I agreed. "I won't keep you—but have you heard the news?"

"What news?"

"Ariel Kominski, of the Komin's grocery store titans died in her bathtub. The same Ariel that lives, or rather, lived, in my townhome complex. She was murdered."

"No!" she gasped. "Let's do Popov's tomorrow."

"Sounds good. What time?"

"Anytime that works for you."

"Can I get back to you?" My mind was on overload with surveys, the wine tasting gig, and the prospect of another dead body, Ariel's. This time, a murder. Popov's seemed like a welcome oasis of sanity.

"No problem."

We signed off with the promise to get together the next day and I went back to work.

Positioned outside the food court, I kept a wary watch for the sheriff. It was dangerously close to the electronics store where he'd ventured from before. My heart skipped a beat when I saw a man with a sturdy build, and silver-streaked, tousled blond hair exit a shoe store adjacent to the food vendors. I held my breath as he glanced my way. I chilled when it wasn't the sheriff and the man disappeared into a sea of shoppers.

As the night wore down, I was grateful when a gray-haired woman I approached answered all my survey questions, saying, "Gosh, this was fun—where can I get a job doing this?" I told her where to apply and she darted off to the research office.

I nearly blurted out, "Have you heard anything about an investigation into bodies left in vacant houses, or Ariel Kominski's death?" and decided not to burst her bubble. Let her meet Jennifer.

I dragged in later in the evening, my calves aching, and sore feet.

I glanced at the kitchen and living room as I went to my bedroom. Boots followed me, meowing. I undressed, put on jammies, washed my face, brushed my teeth, and slipped under the covers.

I woke with a start, all senses on high alert. The time on the clock blinked 2:07 a.m.

Someone was moving in the living room. I held my breath in the darkness until I heard cursing as an intruder stumbled into an unfamiliar object.

"Eddy! Is that you?" I jumped out of bed, and ran to the living room where he was making himself at home on my sofa.

"What the hell, Eddy? Do you know what time it is?"

"Hey, wifey. You left the door open for me," he protested, his lazy brown eyes smiling as he regarded me.

"I did not!" I yelled, jumping up and down in my pink pajamas, waving my arms for emphasis. "I am not your wifey! You have to go!"

I'm getting one of those bars that stops the patio slider from opening. Mentally, I kicked myself for leaving the slider ajar while I put away the groceries. Given we already had a murder in the townhouse complex, it was a dumb thing to do.

"I don't have anywhere else to go," Eddy said in a melancholy voice, not at all like Eddy, the womanizer.

"What do you mean?" staring, my shoulders tense.

"Lola threw me out. This time, for good. My company canned me. My unemployment checks are done."

I stared at Eddy for a full minute. "I'll put the coffee on."

"No coffee for me," Eddy said. "Tea, please."

I went to the kitchen. Eddy had a family a lot like mine, which is to say, none. My mother, a vagabond hippie lived in a commune. I hadn't heard from her in a couple of years. My father died a decade earlier. I have no siblings—none I know of. Eddy's parents were both dead. He was an only child. That was part of our pull. We were essentially orphans. But it didn't mean he could run rampant through my life and my home. I didn't hate Eddy the way I once did. I had had a great marriage with Jake. Our union went a long way towards healing the pain from marriage to Eddy, and discovering he was "commitment challenged."

Maybe not commitment, "fidelity challenged" was more to the point. Eddy had the morals of an alley cat. I steeled my emotions while I put tea bags into mugs and carried them to the sofa.

'Don't let his problems become yours,' I heard Myra's voice in my head, warning me.

"You're a mush," I said, grumbling to myself.

After Eddy and I talked, I learned he wasn't quite as destitute as he'd led me believe. He had lost his marriage and job. Neither were good. But there was a chance his unemployment benefits would be extended. Not much, but something to work with.

"You can stay here until your unemployment benefits kick in, while you look for work," I said, uneasy, as I made the deal. Eddy's history of following through was marginal. I could be stuck supporting him if I showed any mercy.

"Okay, thanks, Katie," he agreed sleepily. "You're the best."

"I mean it," I warned him, "I can't afford to keep you. I can barely afford me and Boots."

"Sure thing," he replied, as he stretched out on the sofa and fell asleep, his snores echoing through the townhouse. I marveled at how fast he could conk out. *Maybe it wouldn't be so awful having company.* I sipped my tea, observing him. Then I heard the decibel level of Eddy's snoring. It could break the sound barrier. *He'd better get a job soon.*

I carried the cups to the kitchen, stowed them in the dishwasher, and grabbed Boots. "Traitor," I whispered. The cat had nestled into the sofa next to Eddy's head. I took him with me feeling like Scarlett in *Gone with the Wind*: *I'll think about it tomorrow*. I shut the bedroom door, blocking Eddy's snores. I slept fitfully the rest of the night, waking every hour on the hour, until the time on the clock said it was time to get up.

I was dressed, and had the coffee brewing the next morning. The smell lured Eddy to the kitchen. I handed him a cup. "I have a few ground rules that I think are important."

"Of course, you do," he groaned, rubbing his eyes, and running his hands through his hair. Taking the mug, he took a gulp.

"Don't get cranky with me."

"Isn't this why we broke up?" he grumbled.

"No. We broke up because of what's her name."

"Oh, yeah," he said, a wide grin creasing his face, his eyes twinkling.

"Not funny."

"Yeah, you're right." He did his best to appear contrite. For Eddy, that was no small accomplishment. "What's up?"

"I won't ask you for rent money, yet. You have to pay for your food, keep your space clean—you can take the spare room for now. The minute you have a job, you're on your own."

"What about the stack of boxes in there? Where do I sleep?" He grinned and batted his lashes at me, teasing.

I ignored the come-on. "You can clean out the bedroom and paint. That will be your rent. Until we figure out a bed, you can sleep on the sofa."

"But I have to look for a job—."

"Getting a job is your primary focus, Eddy," I snapped. "When you don't have an interview; you can work on the room—it's called multitasking." Eddy, with his boyish charm, brought out the drill sergeant part of my father in me.

"Okay, got it." His smile languid, he asked, "What's for breakfast?"

"Cold pizza," I said, frowning. "Go to the store for anything else. I have to go to work. Use this key instead of the patio door," I said, throwing my spare on the counter. "Yeah, yeah, I left it open," I muttered, "I don't need this kind of complication right now," and I left for my new gig, wine hostess.

CHAPTER 18

The wine tasting was scheduled at Grape Vines, a liquor retailer a few miles from home. I had enough time to find a white top, corkscrew, and paper tablecloth at a nearby discount store. I changed from my sweatshirt to the new top in the restroom. Next, I drove to the nearest thrift store to buy a tray to hold samples. It was a blue tag sale, half price. A deal.

I arrived at eleven on the dot for my four-hour shift. This was going to be great. I was pumped.

"Are you the sample lady?" A tall, dark-haired man asked, smiling. He sported a full beard and wore tan slacks with a long-sleeved, yellow, buttoned-down shirt. His sleeves were rolled at the cuff.

"I am."

"I'm Doug. I own the place." He stopped taking bottles of wine out of a box and offered his hand. A gold band gleamed from the ring finger of his left hand. Bummer.

"I'm Katelyn." I shook his hand. His grasp was warm and firm.

"Glad to meet you. We'll set you up there," and he nodded to a table at a corner of the store within sight of the exit.

"Okay, good. I'll get started." I went to the table, covered it with the cloth and busied myself getting bottles of wine for the display. I opened two. I filled store-supplied, sample cups with the new merlot from a

Minnesota vineyard, that Roxy and Meg had raved about.

"That's enough," Doug said, as I started to open a third bottle.

"Yeah." I stopped, putting the corkscrew down.

"You'll have to drink any left-over wine," he grinned, the corners of his eyes creasing.

"Okay." Another benefit.

"Any questions?"

"Restroom?"

"In back, through the 'employees only' door," and he motioned. I looked in the direction he pointed and noted the brown-colored door.

"Okay." I was ready. I'd poured enough samples to cover the bottom of the tray. Doug went to his post at the cash register. About 11:30, people entered at a brisk clip, on a mission during lunch. I offered up samples and customers greedily drank them. I opened another bottle. Most had little comment. A few gave sour expressions after taking a sip.

During a lull, I tasted the red wine. Choking, I twisted away and spit it back in the cup. Quickly, I covered my mouth with one hand, and started to smile at a woman who was busy eyeing the samples. It was the woman from the open house. What was she doing here?

I gagged again, gasped, and muttered, "Sorry, tickle in my throat," and hid my face. I beat it to the restroom.

In the restroom, I rinsed the remnants of the wine with a gulp of water from the spigot. I wiped my mouth with paper towels and freshened my lipstick. I grabbed a few paper towels, opened the door, and observed the table.

The woman moseyed away, plastic cup in hand. The coast was clear. I went back to the table, placing the spare towels to the side of the tray. I kept my head averted, hair covering the sides of my face as I filled more cups, and sporadically peered around, keeping a wary watch.

"This stuff tastes like vinegar!" The spiky, blue-haired woman slapped her empty cup on the table, ignoring the waste basket.

"Red wine is an acquired taste."

"Huh?" She looked at me. "You got any white?"

"Not today," I said, avoiding her glare.

"You look familiar." I felt her study my face, hair, and blouse.

"I get that a lot." I straightened up and faced her straight on, noting her silver-studded eyebrow twitch. Her gaze was sharp, eyes narrowed. We confronted each other in a stare-down.

"Huh!" She snatched the open bottle of merlot from the table, and sprinted away.

"Stop!" I yelled. "Put that bottle back!" and I started after her. She turned around, wine bottle in hand, and hooked the leg of the table with her right leg, and jerked the display. I stopped the chase, and spun around to stop cascading bottles and wine samples as she ran past Doug at the register. I kept the bottles from falling while Doug finished ringing up a customer. He joined me in cleaning up.

"Nice save," he commented, as he up-righted the supply.

"Thanks. I'm sorry. She's a wacko," and I blotted the spilled wine with toweling. "I've seen her before."

I wondered if she had any connection to the bodies in the vacant houses, or if she was just psycho, bent on making my life miserable.

"Uh huh, she's a regular." Resigned, he straightened the bottles of merlot. Miraculously, none had broken, but wine from sample cups covered the floor in a sticky red goo.

"I'll get more towels," I said, relieved I wasn't the only person this woman had tormented, I darted off.

"Bring the mop!" Doug yelled out.

In the restroom, I quickly blotted my blouse, grabbed more towels, dampening a few to absorb the wine. I seized the mop. When I returned, Doug was back at the register ringing out customers. I finished cleaning up the mess, discarding plastic cups and swabbing the floor.

"I think you should call it a day," Doug called at three p.m. My shift was over. The steady traffic had dwindled to a couple of customers in the store. Doug was intent, focused on his cellphone and avoiding eye contact.

I grabbed my tray, corkscrew, and handbag. I felt my face flush, likely matching the stains on my blouse. I fairly ran out of the store. I went straight home, changed, and called Myra, "You wouldn't believe the day I've had," I grumbled when she answered.

"How about we meet at Popov's and you can tell me all about it. Five o'clock?"

"Excellent!" I could hardly wait. But, first I had to clean my blouse.

CHAPTER 19

Amid scrubbing the wine-stained blouse with a mixture of Dawn dishwashing soap and hydrogen peroxide in the bathroom sink, and grumbling to myself and Boots about the day's events, I heard Eddy's key in the lock. Once inside, he flipped on the radio and cranked the volume to deafening levels.

Finished with my chore, I found him in the middle of the living room sifting through a box. He sat on the floor, his back propped against the sofa while he sorted, a can of cola at his side.

"What are you doing?" I switched off the radio.

"Doing what you said to do, make my keep." He got up.

"I didn't say living room—I said bedroom. That bedroom!" I added exasperated, as I nudged him towards the room.

"All right. All right." Eddy hesitated, reached down, and grabbed the cola and radio.

"Yikes! You got a lot of stuff!" he yelled at the entrance to the room. I'd thrown things into hastily labeled boxes when I'd moved.

"Don't forget, painting is part of the deal," I warned Eddy in a nagging tone I fell into more quickly than I wanted. With Eddy in the spare room, I looked at my watch. There was time before meeting Myra.

I rummaged through a closet where I'd stored left-over paint and other painting paraphernalia. The remainder from the Bluebird house would work.

Satisfied, I found two gallons I hadn't used for my rehab house. Beggars couldn't be choosers—it would be fine in the spare bedroom. Although different, the colors were both neutrals, and anything at all would freshen the room. I put the paint aside.

Eddy had stacked unpacked boxes in a corner of the spare room. I stopped him while he assembled an ancient bed. Although I'd rather have an office than another bedroom, the bed frame and mattress was a lucky keep. It meant Eddy could sleep in a bed instead of surprising me on the sofa.

"Hey!" I yelled over the din of the radio.

"What?" He stopped assembling the frame and cupped his ear.

I found the radio and turned the volume down.

"I have paint."

"What?" He started to protest, but stopped when he saw my expression. "Oh, paint. Great." he appeared gloomy.

"Good answer. Follow me."

Eddy straightened, put the metal bed frame aside and trailed me to the painting supply stockpile.

I grabbed a gallon of flat interior latex paint, labeled 'blissful beige' and handed the can to him. "This is your color. If you run out, there's another, 'almond breeze' for the rest. Just paint into the corner when you change cans." I grabbed a roller, dust rags, drop cloth, paint tray, and masking tape.

"I'll move the boxes." I nodded towards the stack, "while you start prepping, I'll go through them."

"Oooh, I love a woman who knows what she wants." He grinned, lifted his brows, and fluttered his eyelashes. If we hadn't been unhappily married at one time, I would have swooned at his charm. Eddy put the cans of paint in a corner of the room and I added the supplies. He laid the drop cloth and wiped the baseboard before masking off the mopboards.

I toted boxes from the bedroom into the living room while Eddy worked. Boots scrambled from his perch as I commandeered part of the sofa. When all the boxes were in the living room, I stood back and surveyed them, eight in all.

"One box a day should do it." I read the first box, 'vacation photos.'

My plan was to put items in the built-in shelves that lined one wall. Once I opened a box, it would take me to another time with Jake. I braced myself. I opened the top box, plucked out an album and parked on the sofa. I leaned back into the couch, holding the scrapbook to my chest, closed my eyes and took a deep breath. It hit me; Jake was gone. I put the album back. I wasn't ready. I carried the boxes to my bedroom. Shoving clothes aside, I stacked them in a corner of the walk-in closet. It would have to do.

I was meeting Myra at Popov's soon, and wanted to check on my house.

I looked in on Eddy. The radio was on full blast and the music reverberated. Music blared as Eddy painted one side of the room. "How do you like me now?" he sang with gusto, along with Toby Keith on the radio.

"Good grief," I said, laughing. Eddy's voice was off-key and out-of-sync with Toby's gravelly voice.

"Gotta go!" I yelled, tapping my watch.

"See ya, wifey," Eddy responded, winked, and continued his rendition of the country song, his long arms painting to the beat of the music.

"I am NOT your wifey!" I shouted over the music. If Eddy heard me, he didn't give any sign. "Good grief, what have I gotten myself into?" I murmured, shutting the door.

I headed to my car, keys in hand, the straps of my handbag thrown over my shoulder. At my vehicle, I stopped while opening the driver's side door and surveyed the parking lot.

Ariel's Jaguar was hooked to a tow truck. There was no sign of Paul. He had been driving the car the night of Ariel's murder. Apparently, he hadn't made the lease payments either. I made a quick detour past my rehab house on the way to Popov's. All was quiet. No news, was good news.

Precisely at five o'clock, Myra and I met. We had a few minutes of chit chat and ordered our favorite, Popov's Burgers and French fries washed down with a glass of wine.

I decided to spare her the latest adventure of quick cash employment. I wasn't sure if Doug would want me back, or if I was still employed as a wine sample person. No need to dwell on it. It was a puzzle why the spiky, blue-haired woman appeared randomly, but one calamity at a time. Doug had said she was a regular. It had to be a coincidence. I focused on Eddy.

"Eddy showed up last night. He's unemployed. Lola kicked him out."

"Oh great." She groaned. Myra knew our history.

"Yeah." I shook my head. "But you first," I said, and sipped the chardonnay. "How's the camera?"

"Well, it's interesting. I have the culprit on film," and she took a sip from her glass.

"You're kidding?" and I waited for her to explain.

"No. I have photographs," she said. "It's a federal crime now," she added, carefully setting her drink on a coaster.

"Federal! How?" My mouth was open while my hands cradled my glass.

"They've been tampering with my mail. That—" She tapped the table firmly with her pointer finger, "—is a federal offense."

"Oh."

"The thief is reaching into my box and taking mail." Myra lived in a neighborhood where mail delivery was door to door. In my neighborhood, delivery was by vehicle to boxes at the curb.

"You are kidding me. You've GOT to be kidding." I was dumbfounded. It seemed unbelievable that in her neighborhood, people would stoop to stealing mail. Myra reached into her handbag, and pulled out a packet of photos. She laid them out in front of her.

"Those are the pictures?" I caught a glimpse of a blurry figure in the pictures spread out across from me.

"Yes. These are still photos from the film with the wreath culprit." She pointed to a grainy photo of a young male in motion. I leaned over to get a better look. It was a side view of the youngster with little detail. Sure enough, the figure had a hand in her mail box, but was moving so fast the camera hadn't captured a clear image.

"Him?" I picked up the picture and squinted. "Do you know this kid?"

"No."

"Okay. Do you think anyone could be identified from this picture?" I asked, squinting at the photograph.

"Not likely. I have some ideas the police could use, but they don't seem interested," she said in a brittle sounding voice.

"All right." She was upset. It wasn't like Myra. Normally, she was calm, cool, and collected. She had a plan and followed through. Things fell into place in her carefully-ordered life.

"The investigator said I could question the neighbors, ask if this was their son, or whether they knew who it was. But, it wasn't a serious enough offense for them to handle themselves." She sounded miffed, and a little embarrassed.

"Oh." I took the last gulp of wine.

"Why would I go to my neighbors and make a stink, if the police don't think it's worth their time?" she demanded.

"Got ya." I signaled the waitress. "I'll have another glass of white wine," I said, and nodded to Myra.

"Make it two," she said, exasperated. She gathered the photos, put them in the envelope and stuffed them back in her purse. When the waitress came back with our chardonnays, I held up my glass.

"To better days," I said, and tipped the glass towards her.

"No kidding." She touched her glass with mine.

With that, I vowed to get back on track with selling the house, and getting to the bottom of the dead body mystery.

CHAPTER 20

We met up again at the Bluebird Street house Saturday morning before our Sunday showing. Myra stepped out of her SUV, wearing a navy-blue blazer, a blue and white patterned silk scarf draped around her neck, and dress slacks. Buff for our walk-through. I wore my usual sweatshirt and jeans, and thought her scarf likely cost more than my entire outfit, sneakers included. If she noticed, I couldn't tell.

The house appeared in good condition, despite being the site of an unfortunate body disposal. It was early May and the lawn was greening up. Tulips and daffodils were popping in a small sunny area under the picture window. New black house numbers, in a script style lettering, stood out beside the freshly painted front door. *This could be the weekend we sell this baby.*

"This looks marvelous," Myra said, as I opened the door.

"It does, doesn't it? Our cleansing ritual did the job."

"Maybe."

We took our time, and strolled the living room, kitchen, bedrooms, bathroom, and headed to the lower level.

"This space is great," Myra remarked. "It will be perfect for a young family. Plenty of room to socialize, watch television, or play games."

Wayne had painted the cement floor and I added a carpet remnant to warm the area. The frieze had texture, style, and durability for a new owner. Who I hoped would come soon, and overlook any pesky problems like finding a body in the attic.

"The colors are wonderful!" she added. "It will sell the house."

"I hope you're right." I'd painted the laundry area a bright sunflower yellow, and used light hues in the rest of the basement.

"It's a great house," Myra said firmly.

"It is."

We left out the front door. I closed up while Myra waited.

"New locks?" she asked.

"Yep." The grim thought of who might have gained entry by the old locks made the expense and change necessary.

"Any news on Ariel?" she asked, as we paused, finished with closing.

"None I know of." I added, "Ariel was quite the puzzle."

"Why is that?"

"Remember how I was put off by her comments about my food choices?"

"Can't blame her. Your pizza, coffee, and cola diet are going to catch up with you, you know," Myra said, chuckling.

"Yeah, yeah, yeah." I rolled my eyes, "I wasn't the only one Ariel gave unsolicited advice to. She gave Mrs. Gilman the business about growing flowers instead of food in her containers. She gave Wayne guff about AA, saying he should kick alcohol addiction on his own, and stiffed him for a shelf."

"So, you are saying one of them killed Ariel?" Myra was skeptical, and brushed her hair from her face.

"No. I'm saying if she put down people she hardly knew—what was she like with people she was intimate with?"

"Like her boyfriend?" Her brows raised.

"Paul was angry with her for spending so much money—she was about to lose her car and townhouse." I slipped the house keys in my purse.

"How do you know she was broke?"

"That gem came from Mrs. Gilman who heard them fighting through paper thin walls—say, do you know a good insulation contractor?" I was obsessed about how much Mrs. Gilman, or anyone else could hear through the walls in the complex.

"Do you think it was her boyfriend?" Myra ignored my last question.

"Don't know. Another thing, why would a health nut like Ariel be smoking marijuana?"

"Marijuana?" she asked, sounding surprised.

"Uh huh. Mrs. Gilman smelled what she thought was weed when Paul was visiting. A visit which sounded amorous, if you know what I mean?"

"Uh huh." She nodded. "Perhaps marijuana was an alternative to alcohol?"

"No, an addition to alcohol," I said. "There was a bottle of champagne—generic champagne chilling the night she died."

"Generic champagne? I've never heard of such a thing."

"Not generic, but a brand claiming to be close to the more expensive Dom Perignon.

"It's a tough economy," Myra conceded, asking, "You're saying, Ariel was a hypocrite?"

"To the max." We reached the end of the sidewalk. "Let's meet a few minutes before the showing," I suggested, adding, "I ran the ad in Sunday's metro paper."

"Sounds good," she agreed and we started for our cars. My dusty Ford wagon was parked behind Myra's SUV, gleaming with polish.

"Are you still using your security camera?" I asked, an afterthought as we parted ways.

"No," Myra said, spitting indignantly. "This time they took the camera."

"Oh no!" I said, ready to open my car door.

"Yes," she said, in a grim tone. "They got it before I could check the new film. I will get them. Somehow, sometime," she vowed, with a tight smile, stepping up to her vehicle.

"You go, girl," I urged, chuckling. *Myra's life isn't so perfect*. Then, I felt guilty.

I waved as she drove away in her SUV. Once she was gone, I got in my Ford and pulled out. I had a little time before I needed to be anywhere. I wanted to take stock of the neighborhood and pick the best locations for open house signs.

The block was quiet in the morning hours. Residents were sleeping in or had gone on about their business of the day. Houses were closed up, with an occasional car in the driveway. The streets were empty.

As I drove, I saw a long vehicle behind me in the rearview mirror. The driver loitered, traveling slowly, stopping at a stop sign. It was a mere two blocks from my Bluebird Street house. "That looks funny," I muttered, as I pulled over to the curb, and let a black hearse pass. The vehicle continued up the street.

A shockwave hit me when I recognized the car. It was the same one that was at Mr. Randal's funeral home with a dented front fender.

I pulled back onto the deserted street and followed the big car at a discreet distance. The hearse stopped, and backed up the driveway of a home advertised as "sold" on the lawn sign. I drove past, averting my gaze. Parking a few yards from the driveway where the hearse had stopped, I flipped my visor down and angled it to capture the scene. I sat and watched the action through the vanity mirror.

Why would a hearse go to an empty house? Curious, I observed. Unless? The hairs rose on the back of my neck as I saw Mr. Randal leap out, stride to the front door and open the metal lockbox that held the key to the house. He opened the entry door, put the key back, and signaled to his passenger.

My jaw dropped when I saw Paul Seever, Ariel's beau, with his unmistakable greasy, duck-tail styled hair, and short muscular build, hop out. Both men gave the appearance of business as usual. They wore business suits, white shirts, and dark ties, appearing professional and unflappable.

Paul went to the rear of the hearse and opened the back door. Mr. Randal met him at the car. The open doors obstructed my view. As I craned my neck to view around the door, the two men hoisted a gurney with a sheet-covered form into the house.

"Oh, my God," I whispered and gasped, my heart racing with a jolt of adrenalin. The men hustled out of the house with the empty gurney and stowed it in the back in the hearse.

Slamming the doors, they sped away. It took all of about a minute in broad daylight. If I hadn't seen it myself, I wouldn't have believed it.

"Oh, crap." I groaned, shaking with excitement. I made a sharp U-turn, followed the car while fumbling for my cell phone.

In a burst of speed, Mr. Randal threw a flashing rotating emergency light on the roof of the hearse. He blasted the horn as he ran the red light. Tires squealing, the car zipped away. I stopped, glared at the red traffic signal, and called Myra.

"Myra, you're not going to believe what I just saw! Mr. Randal and Paul Seever, Ariel's beau—left a body at a vacant house!" and I rattled off the address.

"I'm on my way. I'll call Sheriff Don," she promised, sharply inhaling.

I returned to the house where Randal and Seever had left the body, and waited for Myra and the sheriff to arrive. I got out my cell phone and dialed the number on the realtor's sign.

"How'd they get in?" the sheriff asked as he approached the house. Another officer waited with the squad car. I stood outside the front entry, my arms crossed, biting my bottom lip.

"Randal knew the box combination! He must have! He twisted the dials and bingo—they were in!" I was shaken from what I'd just witnessed and chasing Mr. Randal and Paul Seever.

"I'll call the realtor. It's not breaking and entering if they had a key," Sheriff Don said. He studied me. "I think you need to settle down." I felt my face get hot with frustration and bit back any commentary. Getting mouthy with the sheriff wouldn't help the situation.

"I already called the realtor," I countered. Just then, Myra drove up, got out and joined us on the steps.

At the same time, a man driving a black Land Rover pulled up to the front curb and got out. He was short with receding brown hair and well-dressed.

"I'm the realtor." He introduced himself to the sheriff. We moved, letting him at the lockbox. He entered the code. Once open, he handed the key to the sheriff.

"How could someone get the combination to the box if they didn't own the house, and didn't work for the realty company?" Sheriff Don asked, his stern gaze fixed on the realtor.

"Well, I don't know," he stammered. "I know I didn't give anyone the combination. But the locks aren't difficult to pick," he said, gulping. The bald spot on his head shone and sweat dripped down the sides of his face. He wiped his face with a handkerchief from his coat pocket. Flustered by the sheriff, he protested, "Anyone can research the internet and see how it's done. I don't want any trouble. The house is sold. I don't want any trouble," he repeated, adding, "It's a foreclosure. No one lives there."

"You don't say," the sheriff said. "The internet?"

"Well," the agent said, his complexion red, "Everything's online now. Whether it's legal or not…"

"Uh huh," the sheriff said, and gave him a sidewise gaze.

"Look," the man said, blotting droplets of perspiration, "I've never had any problems before. The new owner asked me to leave the box with a key so workmen could get in."

The agent had a point. Rather than leave a key with different tradespeople, it was common to have a key in the lockbox for workers going in and out.

"Give your contact information to the officer before you leave. I'll need the name of the new owner," the sheriff instructed the agent.

"Yes, sir." The man paled under the request. Emergency vehicles arrived and crime scene investigators hurried into the house. I felt a blast of cold air from the house's air conditioning through the open door.

"Doesn't make much sense to me," Sheriff Don muttered, rubbing his chin as they entered the house. "A funeral home is paid to bury the man."

Myra and I cleared the sidewalk while two men carried the body to a county vehicle. We averted our eyes while they loaded the body. Sheriff Don joined us, silent. The CSI people slammed the van's doors, hopped in the transport, and drove off. Sheriff Don went to the agent who stood to one side, his mouth agape.

Myra and I watched as the sheriff grilled the agent again about the lock box.

"The house closed yesterday," I overheard the man say. "I left the key in the lockbox after the closing. If Mr. Randal got in quickly, he must have had the code or picked the lock."

It wasn't such a stretch. If Mr. Randal had enough guts to leave a body, picking a lock would be a walk in the park. I wrote down the name of the agent and realty company on a wad of paper plucked from my purse. Sheriff Don, finished with the agent, strolled over to Myra and me.

"What if the mortuary had been paid for burying the body?" I asked Sheriff Don, recalling how poor the accounting system was at Colossal Health. When they merged with a smaller hospital, they paid two or three times for the same billing. At other times, they paid nothing for legitimate charges. One system didn't talk to the new system, fighting with different software, causing multiple headaches for staff and patients alike.

"What do you mean?" Sheriff Don asked.

"I mean," I said, "hypothetically, would it be possible for the funeral home to collect twice for the same burial?" I went on. "If these were charity cases, with no relatives or friends to vouch for them, or to attend a funeral—who would know whether the morgue was paid for burying these people?"

"I see what you mean, Katelyn," he admitted.

"Yee gads," Myra burst in, "I know times are tough, but that would be terrible, not to mention fraudulent, at the very least."

"Unlawful disposal of a body and a whole host of other charges," the sheriff agreed.

"But what about Jimmy Woo, the first man found?" Myra asked. "He had relatives. They came to our first open house."

"I don't know." I shook my head, shrugging, "His burial was paid for by the county."

"Katelyn, don't leave town," Sheriff Don cautioned. "You were the first to report this. I'll take you at your word that Mr. Randal and his hearse were here, and left the body at this house. We will investigate. But it seems a mite suspicious that only you saw this happen. It's going to be his word against yours."

He got into his patrol car and drove off in the same direction of the crime scene vehicles. Once again, yellow tape cordoned off the entry.

"Oh great," I groaned to Myra after Sheriff Don left. "I'm a suspect again."

"Let me call my brother," Myra said, consoling me.

"Okay," I said, brightening, "It couldn't hurt."

I got into my trusty wagon, leaving Myra at her SUV. I was running late for my shift at the research mall. Jennifer was going to throw a fit.

CHAPTER 21

I called Jennifer pleading a migraine and asked to come in later. It wasn't a total lie. My head did throb from the morning's events.

I stopped at Wayne's door before I headed to mine. I filled him in on what had transpired, and repeated what Sheriff Don said about being the sole witness to Mr. Randal and Paul Seever leaving the body at a vacant house.

"Kiddo, you don't have a thing to worry about! You were in the wrong place, wrong time, or right place at the right time. Depends on how you look at it!" he ranted, his pony tail flying as he shook his head, and let me into his foyer.

"Thanks, Wayne; I hope you're right." I couldn't help worrying. It was my nature. Changing the subject, I asked, "You wouldn't happen to have a long thin piece of wood? Like a dowel, or a strip of sturdy wood, about yay long?" I walked to his kitchen slider, and held my arms wide showing the length.

"Like a burglar bar? You got problems with intruders, kiddo?" he quizzed me with a worried expression.

"Not anymore," I said, thinking about the arrangement I had with Eddy. "Let's just say I have a roomie for a while."

"Okay, kiddo, no need to explain nothing to me," he winked.

"Wayne, it's not like that," I protested. "Eddy, my ex, is staying with me until he gets his feet on the ground. I'd feel safer. Should have gotten one a long time ago."

"A roomie or a burglar bar?" Wayne asked, and chuckled. "Sure, kiddo, I've got something in the garage that'll work. I'll bring it over."

I went home. All was quiet. Eddy had left a note saying he was checking out a job.

"Uh huh, I'll bet." Still, it was nice he left a note. It made me feel all warm and fuzzy inside. With the peace and quiet, I slipped off my shoes to nap with Boots on the sofa.

Rat a tat! Wayne's knock came. After a quick check through the peephole, I opened the door. True to his word, he held up a one-by-two piece of lumber, cut to length.

"Perfect!"

"You sleeping?" he asked, observing my hair.

"Napping." I smoothed my mane with one hand.

"Sorry."

"No, no problem." I let him in. He went to the slider and slipped the lumber between the tracks and tried the door. The wooden bar held the door firmly.

"Thanks, Wayne." I pulled the length of wood out of the opening and put it aside.

"Glad to help," he said with a grin. He was about to leave when there was a loud knock at the door. I opened it to find Sheriff Don.

"I'll have to take you in, Katelyn," he said, grimly. Wayne stood beside me, stunned.

"Good grief. Why?" I asked.

"We'll discuss it at the station."

"You go ahead, kiddo," Wayne urged. "I'll follow you; see if I can do anything."

I slipped into my shoes and grabbed my handbag. The sheriff ushered me to a waiting squad car. He opened the back door and motioned me in.

A glance around the interior of the cruiser told me if I tried to run, there were no door handles. The window which separated passengers from the driver appeared solid. The seat was firm, no cushy ride here. There was nothing to do except sit back. I attempted to relax under the watchful eye of Sheriff Don while he studied me carefully through the rearview mirror on the drive to the station.

He drove into the police station's lot, parked, came to the back of the cruiser, and opened the door. I stepped out. He slammed the door, a grim look on his face. Silently, he motioned me to precede him and headed to his office. Once there, he pointed to a chair and I sat gingerly and waited, my stomach in knots.

Seated behind his desk, Sheriff Don fixed his sharp gaze on me, his deep, blue eyes sparking with anger.

"Katelyn, I'll make this quick," he said. "I talked to Mr. Jackson Randal this morning and he denies being anywhere near the house where we found the body. He asked me to describe the person who made the complaint. He said a woman who fit the description was at his funeral home earlier in the week with a man. The couple claimed they were making arrangements for the man's wife, who was a sick aunt of the woman. He became suspicious because the female appeared to be snooping. Can you deny that, Katelyn?" he demanded, his voice rising in anger.

"Maybe," I said, evading the question.

"Do you have an ill aunt?" Sheriff Don asked, getting more agitated. "Was it you at Mr. Jackson Randal's funeral home?"

"Yes, I was there," I admitted, stalling for time, "but I wasn't snooping. I needed to use the restroom." My cell phone rang. Sheriff Don glared while I dug it out of my purse.

"I'll get it!" he said, reaching for the phone and snatching it from my hand. Speechless, I watched him.

"This is Sheriff Williams," he snapped.

I heard his side of the conversation as I sat twiddling my thumbs. *This is a fine mess I've gotten myself into.*

"Uh huh; okay, Myra. I'll do that. Say 'hi' to your brother for me." He disconnected and handed the phone to me. He leaned back, and said, "Your friend Myra called the police chief. He called the transportation department. They pulled the film from the camera at the intersection where you reported seeing the hearse run the stop light. The video shows the vehicle running the red light, like you said. But," he emphasized, "the photo doesn't prove Mr. Randal was driving." He conceded, grudgingly, "the car is registered to the mortuary."

"So, I can go?" I asked, breathing a sigh of relief, and standing up.

"You can go for now. But don't go playing private detective on me again," he warned. "There could be something more to this than meets the eye. Our office is handling it." His manner softened; he didn't quite smile, but his eyes sparkled. "You could be charged with impeding an official police investigation."

Wayne, bless his heart, was pacing outside the entrance, waiting for me.

"Need a lift, kiddo?" He winked, and gestured towards his van.

"Thanks, Wayne." I got in and rested my head against the head support.

"Tough morning," he commented, as he put the vehicle in gear. "Home?"

"Home, sweet home," I agreed, closing my eyes with a deep breath.

Back at the townhouse, I gave Boots fresh water and a snack. I put the burglar bar into position before I showered and dressed for my stint at the mall. Jennifer hadn't fired me, yet. The hemorrhoid study had been a bust and she wasn't happy. I was pushing it by going in late, but it couldn't be helped. There weren't any messages on voice mail from the liquor distributor. I could only imagine what Doug had relayed to Roxy and Meg about my stint as a wine sample hostess.

Jennifer put me on a baby food study, deciding I had better rapport with young parents than old geezers. Jennifer was right. I did the highest number of surveys of any researcher that night with young mothers and fathers who extolled the virtues of an all-natural line of baby food. Had my brain suffered as a result of processed baby food? Could that explain my present situation? Doubtful.

It was after nine when I got home from my shift at the research group. I removed the new burglar bar, opened the sliding patio door, and stepped into the night air. I breathed in the clean smell of spring. It was a peaceful and clear evening with the promise of a long summer ahead.

There was no sign of Eddy. Between surveys with parents, I had mused about how it would be going home to a roommate besides Boots. It might have some merit, especially if he got the second bedroom in shape. I went inside, replaced the bar, and headed to the spare room to check out his work. He hadn't finished putting the bed together and it appeared as though he'd left in a hurry, leaving the container of paint open as well as a cola can. He'd have to sleep on the couch again.

I put the lid on the paint can and picked up the discarded beverage. I was in the kitchen when I heard the rattle of a key and Eddy came through the door.

"Wifey, I'm home," he chortled. He looked pleased with himself.

"I told you, I'm not your wife—and you've been drinking." I glared at him. The Eddy I knew, was back.

He ignored my grousing and came to the sink where I rinsed a glass. He put both arms around me and I winced at the acrid odor of beer and cigarette smoke. "I've got an interview in the morning," he said, seeing my reaction.

"Great, Eddy, great." I squirmed out of his hold and faced him, "You'll need to get some rest. What time is the interview?"

"Nine thirty. It's a good job," he crowed.

"Good. I'm going to bed," I said. Taking a glass of water, I scooped up Boots on the way to my bedroom.

"Sweet dreams," Eddy said, mumbling, and heading to the sofa.

I locked my bedroom door in case Eddy got any ideas. I washed my face, brushed my teeth, and put on jammies. After a few restless turns, I was out like a light.

A few hours later, my eyes flew open. I heard noises and all my senses went on high alert. The digital clock on my bedside table glowed 2:05 a.m. I strained to make sense from the sounds coming from the living room.

Thump! I heard an object hit the floor.

"Damn it!" a male voice complained. The voice came again, demanding, "What in the Sam hell?"

"Who's there!" Eddy yelled. Lights went on, visible from the slit under my bedroom door. I hit the lamp switch, jumped out of bed, crept to the door, and listened. Holding my breath, I heard an angry man demand, "WHO THE HELL ARE YOU?" Then, I heard sounds like fists hitting body parts, grunting, and living room furniture being tossed about.

Shaking, I grabbed the hammer from my night stand drawer and rushed back to the door. I unlocked it with one hand while brandishing the hammer in the other. Boots stayed on the bed, wary, among the pillows. I flung open the door and dashed to the living room.

Eddy was in his tidy-whiteys, wrestling Mr. Randal into a chokehold. Randal stood bug-eyed, strands of his thin, greasy hair wild, gasping for breath, while Eddy's arm pressed against his Adam's apple.

"Call the cops!" Eddy yelled.

"I'm on it!" I shouted, wielding the hammer.

I dashed past the living room to the kitchen phone. *Thank goodness, I have a landline.* I didn't know where my cell phone was.

Out of the corner of my eye, I saw Randal's arms thrash and throw Eddy off balance. Randal arched his back. Using every bit of strength with a backward thrust of his leg, he hit pay dirt in Eddy's groin. Eddy groaned, losing his grip on Randal. Randal jerked his torso down, breaking free from Eddy. He ran for the door, fumbled with the deadbolt, twisted the handle and burst into the hall, yelling, "Dammit! Mikey said you lived alone! That SOB!"

"There's an intruder! He's getting away!" I yelled into the phone at the 9-1-1 operator, as Randal ran out the door.

"I have an officer on the way. Stay on the line until help arrives," the dispatcher advised.

"Dammit, Katelyn. What the hell?" Eddy came to the kitchen, shirtless, wearing his skivvies, holding his groin.

"Put some clothes on; the cops are coming!" My mind raced and adrenalin surged.

There was a loud knock at the door.

It was too late for Eddy to get dressed.

"Police! Open up!"

I opened the door. Sheriff Don was standing outside the entry, hand at his holster, ready to take out his firearm.

My stomach lurched.

Sheriff Don studied Eddy. His face was a mask, except for a deepening red, as he took in the scene. I wore pink pajamas and Eddy stood behind me in his undies, still shirtless.

"You reported a disturbance, Ms. Baxter?"

"Some dude broke in!" Eddy said, gasping. "I had him, but he got away!"

"It was Mr. Randal from the mortuary," I said, breathless, smoothing my hair.

"It appears the intruder is gone now." The sheriff cleared his throat. "I was in the area when the call came in. There's another car on the way, Ms. Baxter."

Any random thoughts of a mutual attraction faded as Sheriff Don addressed me with my surname and a veil of formality. Any hint of interest evaporated with his closed expression.

Eddy vanished to the living room, and came back wearing jeans and a tee shirt. I heard sirens in the distance. "Kate, did you know that man?" he asked.

"It was Jackson Randal, the funeral home's director. I'll fill you in," I said, shaken. Sheriff Don, at the door in the middle of the night, added to the trauma of an intruder. Especially with Eddy looking like he'd slept there. Okay, Eddy was sleeping there, but on the couch. A likely story.

"He made one hell of a move," Eddy muttered.

Sheriff Don didn't appear impressed. His body blocked the doorway while he waited for my explanation.

"Yeah, he's a slippery one," I said, remembering Randal's limp handshake and greasy hair. "Thanks, Eddy, I owe you."

Sheriff Don's eyebrows lifted and his brow furrowed. When two officers appeared, he said, "I'll be on my way. These men can help you with your report, Ms. Baxter." He nodded to the policemen, saying, "Appears there was an intruder; they'll fill you in." His shoulders stiff, he threw one last irritated glance at me and left.

While one officer took our statements, the other viewed the disarray in the living room. Eddy sat next to me at the kitchen table while the officer took his report. I told the reporting officer, "I put the burglar bar in place before I left for work, and removed it when I got home. I know I replaced it before I went to bed."

"You look familiar," the officer said, perplexed, as he took notes.

"I have that look," I said, then figured I'd come clean. "I was at the station earlier today. I saw Mr. Randal and another man, Paul Seever, at an empty house disposing of a body. I reported it, and Mr. Randal must have thought my house was the safest place to hide. He had to have entered while I was with the sheriff."

I'd put it together—the thought creeping me out. After Randal had talked to the sheriff, he knew they would be searching for him. He'd gotten in through the unsecured patio door while I was at the station. He must have hidden in the second bedroom while I got ready for work. It was flat out ballsy. He'd bet the police wouldn't search my house. When he was ready to flee in the dead of night, he'd surprised Eddy, asleep on the sofa.

"Mikey told him I lived alone." I repeated what Randal had shouted on his way out.

"It's good you were here," the officer addressed Eddy. "No telling what he would have done."

"Happy to help, wifey," Eddy said, with a smile.

"Your wife is very lucky."

"We're not married. Inside joke," I said. There was a sick feeling in the pit of my stomach, when I considered what could have happened. Randal could have waylaid me, as he hid from the police. It was lucky, I had locked the bedroom door when I went to bed. Would he have killed if he'd been discovered? The thought was sobering.

It was nearly four o'clock, when the police left. I was too wound up to sleep. Eddy didn't have any trouble getting back to sleep. I tossed and turned while Randal's words ran through my mind, checking the time every few minutes, until it was time to get up.

CHAPTER 22

"Mikey said you lived alone!" Randal's words stuck in my brain like an ear worm the next morning. After Eddy went off to his interview in high spirits, I pondered the statement through the morning while I tidied up. Satisfied everything was where it was before the prior night's fiasco, I got ready for the day.

I called Sheriff Don after lunch.

"I'll meet you at Colossal Health," he agreed. After that, I made a few more calls.

I raced to the hospital in my dusty Ford wagon, Myra riding shotgun, clinging to the shoulder strap of the seat belt, her right foot acting as an imaginary brake.

"Kiddo, where'd you learn to drive like this?" Wayne asked from the back seat, as I made a sharp right and floored the accelerator. He gripped the edges of the seat, fighting the momentum to slide from side to side.

"Television!" I retorted, and made a left turn into the parking lot of Colossal Health Hospitals.

"It's him," I said, sharply inhaling. Speechless, we watched as Sheriff Don marched Michael Preston Ness to the waiting police car, all lights flashing.

The big man was cuffed and stumbled as the sheriff herded him to the car. His round face was easily twice as red as the day he and Janice from HR had escorted me out of the building on my last day of work. It was satisfying to see him get his just desserts.

News trucks from all the twin cities television stations, along with the local cable channel, recorded his walk of shame. My calls as a private citizen to news stations reporting "breaking news" had paid off handsomely. I allowed myself a pat on the back. I was still the best marketing facilitator out there.

I'm sure "Mikey" had paid Mr. Randal a nice sum for breaking into my place after I'd witnessed Randal and Paul Seever disposing of the bodies.

"So, what was Mikey's deal in all of this?" Wayne asked, while we sat and watched, entranced by the unfolding scene.

"He got a kickback from Mr. Randal every time he steered someone to his funeral home for burial. Charity cases were best, because there were fewer people paying attention," Myra said. She added with a smile, "It doesn't hurt to have a brother who's the county's police chief."

"But," I said, "Mikey got greedy. He decided they could make more money if they did one voucher, retrieved the body from the casket, and used the body again to obtain another voucher. That way, Randal got two funeral vouchers, and Mikey got double kickbacks. These poor people have no one to advocate for them so the plan was simple."

"It took the pressure off Mikey to wait for another body, and determine who was indigent and unknown and who wasn't. No one caught on. One accounting system didn't talk to the other, so using the same name wasn't a problem. They learned it was a mistake to use someone with known relatives twice in the county system— Jimmy's relatives howled when they were notified of another burial. Most of the notifications came back 'addressee unknown.' It was a wonder his relatives were ever found."

"I can imagine their confusion, kiddo," Wayne said, grimacing.

"Not to mention the fraud to the taxpayers," Myra added.

"The hospital told Jimmy's mother and sister it was a computer glitch. They told them they didn't need to pay anything for his burial or service. That satisfied them until his body showed up in my attic."

"So, what was Paul's motive for doing all of this— was it money, too?" Myra speculated, asking, "Are they arresting him?"

"Sheriff Don said he would send a team to arrest Paul at his mother's place, as we speak," I said. "I wanted to see Michael Preston Ness' arrest go down. It's personal."

"I hear you," Myra said, giving a nod and sidewise glance.

"Ditto," Wayne agreed, giving a thumbs up.

"Paul's motive was something more than money. He was a different kind of bird. He wanted the free and moneyed lifestyle he had with Ariel, along with her family's prestige."

"How high can we fly?" Wayne said, with a laugh and nod.

"Yep," I replied, remembering the scene in Ariel's bathroom the night she died. The bottle I'd presumed was shampoo, resembled the bottles containing embalming fluid in the supply closet of the mortuary. Paul had access to the chemical that was used in "wet" marijuana.

"Paul came back for the bottle of formaldehyde after Ariel's death," I said, adding, "Marijuana and embalming liquid would show up in the bloodwork if they were celebrating."

"We haven't heard the results from the autopsy, have we?" Myra asked. "I'll need to talk to my brother."

Wayne and I groaned aloud when Myra mentioned her brother. Still, it didn't hurt that she knew someone higher in the pecking order.

I left Myra at her home. She got out of my car, stretching, saying she would call with any updates from her brother. Wayne took her place in the passenger's side. I drove home, satisfied with the day's events. Michael Preston Ness had gotten his due. Even better, everyone at the hospital had seen him led from his office in handcuffs to the police cruiser. It would top every local news station's evening newscast.

I stopped in the driveway and let Wayne out. He eased his lanky legs out the car, and I headed to the garage to park.

Mrs. Gilman came out wearing a yellow hoodie and sweat pants, carrying an envelope to post. I closed my garage door and met up with Wayne and Mrs. Gilman on the sidewalk.

"Yo, Gillie," Wayne greeted her, his voice crooning.

"Wayne," she gushed, her face lit up.

"We still on for the movie?" he asked, with a broad smile.

"Yes, Wayne, that will be lovely. Nice to see you, Katelyn." Mrs. Gilman nodded towards me and continued to the postal box.

"Bye, kiddo," Wayne said, and winked, joining her, "Gillie and I are going to grab something to eat, and catch the double feature at the drive-in." The town's one surviving drive-in theatre had started its Friday night fare of double features.

"Have fun, you two." It was spring and love was in the air.

Mrs. Gilman dropped her letter at the mail box. Wayne draped his arm around her shoulder as they strolled to his vehicle. He threw open the passenger's side and held her hand as she stepped up to the van.

I let myself in, thinking about love, Eddy, and missing my beloved Jake. Boots rose from his roost, meowing. I spotted a note from Eddy scrawled on a piece of notepaper left on the kitchen table, "Going out, don't wait up."

"It's just us tonight, Boots." Stroking the cat, I fed him a can of tuna and ordered up my favorite pizza from the local delivery joint. "We're going to celebrate."

I was finishing my third piece of pizza when Myra called.

"My brother said the medical examiner confirmed Ariel was strangled. The pattern on the chain the men found in the drain matched the indentations in Ariel's neck," her voice rose in excitement as she explained.

"Ugh," I said, groaning.

"Whoever strangled Ariel with the necklace, broke the chain, and dropped it! You said she always wore a silver cross?"

"She did." It was hard to miss.

"Whoever has the cross is the murderer! My brother said they were going to search Paul Seever's mother's house and Ariel's car. According to one of your neighbors, Mrs. Gilman, she saw Paul leave Ariel's townhouse with a paper bag the night of the murder. She said it appeared suspicious."

"Call if you hear anything else," I said, and disconnected. My extrasensory perception kicked in. What if the bottle wasn't all Paul came back for? Maybe, he searched for Ariel's chain? He'd taken a couple of minutes and couldn't linger with neighbors milling around. Desperate, he may have taken the bottle because it was obvious, and left without finding the chain.

Following my gut, I slipped on a jacket, tucked my cellphone in my pocket, and grabbed a plastic baggie and a flashlight from the kitchen. Outside, all was quiet in the driveway as I trotted to the garages.

The parking lot lights illuminated the garage doors. I grabbed the handle to Ariel's stall and tugged. It wouldn't budge. I tried the side garage door. I twisted the knob and the door opened with the sound of a high-pitched creak. I clicked on the flashlight to view an empty stall. Ariel's luxury car had been towed. Had it been repossessed? Did Ariel's family have the Jag? Who got Ariel's possessions seemed a minor detail in the chaos of her death.

I shut the door and aimed the flashlight into the corners of the building. In the solitude, I felt my heart pounding. I stilled myself, listening to my sixth sense as I trained the light into crevasses. I paced the length and the width of the stall. A spot of glitter made me halt as I focused the light up and down the open studs of the structure. I sucked in my breath.

It was there. Peeking out, was a tiny gleam of silver. It was at the top of a stud, front and center of the garage. I looked around. How could I reach the top? There was no step ladder.

Gripping the flashlight, I extended my arm as far as it could go, and jumped at the cross. Maybe, I could knock it off the ledge. No dice. It sat, mocking me. Desperately, I inspected the stall. It was at that moment; I spied a one-by-six length of wood propped in a corner of the garage. The wood was likely left over from Wayne's shelving project for Ariel.

I positioned my flashlight on the floor, trained on the silver object, and went for the wood. Hoisting the piece by one end, I aimed. It was shorter by about two feet than what was needed to reach the cross. I lifted my arms taking a swipe at the silver piece, and missed it. The tip of silver sat, scornful of my aim. I took another jab at the shiny object; it stirred an inch. Grunting at the weight of the wood, I extended my arms again, jumping, putting my weight into another thrust.

The silver piece spun around and flew off the edge, bouncing off a wall stud. *Awesome.* It landed at the side of the garage. Grabbing the flashlight, I went to the silver cross. Taking the plastic baggie from my pocket, I bent to scoop up the crucifix gleaming back at me.

Ariel's garage door snapped open. A car's headlights blinded me as the driver revved the engine. Swiftly bagging the cross and stuffing the baggie in my pants pocket, I faced the car. Shielding my eyes, I saw Paul Seever behind the driver's seat of Ariel's Jaguar, his face twisting in rage.

I dashed to one side of the garage; the car narrowly missed me. It squealed to a stop. Seever threw the car into park, flinging open the driver's door, blocking my exit from the garage stall.

More adrenalin kicked in and I scrambled to the side garage door. I breezed out, my breath coming in jagged gasps. I ran to the patio door of my townhouse and kept running, past my patio, past Mrs. Gilman's, to Ariel's patio door.

Miraculously, it was open. I said a prayer, thanking God or whoever was in charge of open doors, and slipped in. Slamming the slider, I ran to Ariel's bedroom closet and hid, crouching, making myself as small as possible. I heard Paul pounding on the door to my house as I snatched my cellphone from my jacket pocket and dialed 9-1-1.

"Nine-one-one. What's your emergency?"

"Come quick, there's a killer pounding at my door!" I whispered hoarsely into the earpiece.

"Could you speak up? Repeat your emergency."

"THERE'S A KILLER POUNDING AT MY DOOR!" I shook with fear, panicked that Paul could come to Ariel's door at any moment.

At that moment, I heard what sounded like a kick and the sound of my townhouse door breaking into a million pieces.

"YOWL!" Boots yelled, "YOWL, YOWL!" My blood started boiling and it felt like my chest would explode. With a surge of adrenalin, I screamed my address to the operator. In the distance, I heard sirens whine. I burst out of Ariel's closet.

"DON'T YOU DARE HURT MY CAT!" I yelled into the dark bedroom. I went for the light switch, gagging with the profusion of lilac and purple colors in the bedroom.

I scanned the room for any kind of weapon. Not much. I strained to hear Paul's movements in my townhouse. It was quiet, too quiet. Then, I spied the wall shelf Wayne had made for Ariel propped against the dresser. I hefted the ornate, sturdy, red oak piece and headed out. I threw open Ariel's entry door.

"BOOTS! COME HERE!"

Boots came barreling out of my townhouse, running towards me. He scampered past me into the safety of Ariel's living room and hid. Paul Seever was a couple feet behind the cat. His face still contorted with fury, the grease holding his slicked-back hair shining eerily from the lighting in the hallway. He held a black revolver.

"YOU BITCH!" He waved the gun at me.

I threw the shelf, aiming for Paul's groin.

He pulled the trigger, pieces of door molding splintered beside my head. I ducked back inside Ariel's townhouse, slamming the door. In a frenzy, I threw the deadbolt.

"OWWWE!" a scream of pain echoed from the other side of the door. Relief swept through me; the weight had hit its target. I slumped against the door. About to peer through the peephole of Ariel's door, Sheriff Don's stern voice ordered, "DON'T SHOOT, PAUL!"

Then I heard the sound of a gun blast.

CHAPTER 23

Paul had put the gun barrel against his temple, and pulled the trigger. The rest of night was a blur.

The next day, the sheriff asked me to come to the station and go through the events.

"Something told me Paul had hid the cross the night Ariel died," I said, accepting a cup of coffee from the sheriff. "He couldn't have the cross on his body with the police around. Besides Ariel's bathroom, he'd been in her car, parked in her garage. He couldn't risk being stopped and searched—so he must have hidden the cross in the first place he found. He just threw it in the rafters. He forgot the formaldehyde and had to retrieve the bottle from her bathroom."

"He figured if he got caught with the formaldehyde— it was a lesser offense than murder. Drug charges wouldn't get him a long stretch behind bars—like killing Ariel would," the sheriff said. "Death was the better route in his mind, than if he got arrested for murder."

"That's true," I nodded. "A murder conviction would mean a long sentence."

"It was still a foolish thing for you to do, Kate. Sheriff Don held my eyes with his own deep blue ones, and I felt my face flush. "You should have called me."

"It was just a hunch." I shrugged, and shifted in my chair across from him. "Too bad Paul showed up while I was searching the garage."

"It was smart you went to Ariel's townhouse—and didn't lead him back to yours," he said.

"I knew he'd come after me. He knew where I lived." I added, "It was a stroke of luck Ariel's patio door was open."

"Dang it!" Sheriff Don muttered, groaning. He leaned back and slapped the side of his head.

"What?"

"I bet the technicians left the door open when they disassembled the drain. They said the unit smelled, so they aired the place out."

"It's possible the lock didn't fully engage. Stuff happens."

"I'll talk to them. Sloppy work. Can't leave a crime scene open to the public," the sheriff grumbled. "They should have checked the door."

"I'm glad they didn't. Or if they did, it didn't open." I paused. "It let me evade Paul." I met the Sheriff's gaze squarely, raising my eyebrows.

"Lucky break," the sheriff agreed, his attitude changed. "Kate, you know best from living in the townhouses. I suppose, they could have shut the door. The latch didn't catch, but the dang door didn't open when they checked it."

"Yep," I agreed. "I'm sure that's what happened."

"That takes care of everything, Kate." His eyes glowed, and his face lit up with a broad smile.

I was rattled, but not so flustered I hadn't noticed it was the third time Sheriff Don had used "Kate" instead of his usual "Katelyn." Or, that he hadn't used the dreadful, "Ms. Baxter," and that he actually smiled at me.

Standing up, my knees buckled, and I felt a rush of blood to my face.

"Maybe you should take a few more minutes." He came around his desk, and put a hand on each shoulder to steady me. My body warmed with the touch of his hands. I gazed up into his eyes and felt my stomach lurch. As my legs regained stability, the moment passed. He let his hands drop.

"You, okay?" He looked away; his voice businesslike.

"Yeah, sure." I shrugged. The air filled with tension. *Get a grip, Katelyn. You must be insane. This is an officer of the law.* For just a moment, a tiny moment, I thought I saw something more in the sheriff's eyes. Something that said I was more than a crazy lady, with dead people showing up around me.

I turned to leave.

"Thanks, Kate. Thank you for your help." I observed the sheriff. His voice was low and his eyes had a twinkle again.

"Not a problem," I said, confused and puzzled. Maybe I wasn't insane—just delusional. It happens with stress.

"Kate! I came as soon as I heard the news!" Myra exclaimed. She surprised me, waiting outside the sheriff's door.

I was never happier to see her, with her perfectly styled hair and designer outfit.

She hugged me, putting her arm around my shoulders, "You need a drink."

"Uh huh, a stiff drink, or a very large glass of wine."

"Let's go. Sheriff?" Myra viewed the sheriff. He stood at the doorway, and studied the two of us. "Is there anything else?"

"No, ma'am." He shook his head. "Kate, I'll be in touch."

The gears appeared to turn inside Myra's head. "Kate?" she whispered into my ear as we left.

"I know." I looked at her, bewildered. "He started calling me Kate and being all friendly."

"See what happens when you're a little nicer," Myra crooned, a satisfied smile on her face. "He's a good man."

"I think he was just happy to wrap up Ariel's murder," I said, dismissing any romantic interest.

"You helped him with that. My brother will be pleased."

"Harrumph," I replied, glancing at her. "I need wine. Let's get a drink."

When we got to Popov's, we found a booth and ordered a bottle of chardonnay. I drank most of it; thankful Ariel's killer was gone for good.

CHAPTER 24

It was Sunday morning. Myra and I were at the Bluebird Street house preparing for the showing. She could tell I was cautious after our last open and gave me a pep talk.

"Everyone is a potential buyer, and we all have to live somewhere. Someone may as well buy your house. You would be doing them a favor." Her words cheered me.

Shortly after we opened the home, a young couple entered with two young girls. One girl appeared to be about two or three. The other was a baby, wearing a pink bonnet, gripping a binkie, and carried by her father. The three-year old held her mother's hand as the couple examined the renovated house. The woman took a spec sheet and showed it to the man.

"I think we can even afford this house." He grinned at the young woman.

He went to the basement while she toured the main level with the toddler. "Honey, there's new carpeting in the basement," the man yelled. The woman followed his voice to the lower level and said, "Oh, that will be great for the girls!"

Myra and I looked at one another as we waited in the kitchen. I whispered, "These people seem normal."

"I told you so," she replied, smiling, her voice low and hushed.

"At last!" I grinned at Myra while the couple with their young children went through the house, oohing and loving everything from the layout to the color pallet. I heard the happy sounds of money going into my bank account, instead of out. In a burst of optimism, I took sales forms from my messenger bag.

"Would you like to put an offer on the home?" I asked the couple when they finished their inspection.

They glanced at each other. The man said, "It's a strong contender. There are a couple of other houses in the neighborhood we wanted to see. Can we take your card?"

"Sure." I masked my disappointment. They had been so excited. "I could call later to see how your home shopping went and answer any other questions you might have?"

"No. No, that's okay," he said, adding, "We'll call you."

"Sure." I handed him my business card.

"I'll call you," the man promised, as he accepted my card.

"We love the house," the woman said, with a huge smile, lifting her little girl into her arms.

"I'm happy you do. Thank you for stopping by." I escorted the couple to the door.

"They'll be back. You'll see," Myra said, assuring me.

"I hope so. I'd sure like to give up that market research gig." Meg and Roxy from the liquor distributor hadn't called.

I collected the brochures and stuffed them into my bag at the close of the open house. The house locked, Myra and I started for our vehicles. It was then a van caught my attention, driven by a familiar face. We both paused, watching the vehicle pass, mesmerized by the name emblazoned across the side, "Prize Patrol."

"Myra," I gasped. "It's Dave Sayer—and the prize patrol van!"

"The what?" Myra was perplexed. The van slowed.

I had never divulged my obsession for winning a Publisher's Clearing House Prize. One of the prizes promised $5,000 a week for life. It was my little daydream. To win PCH sweepstakes and never do consumer research again.

"Hey, Dave! Over here!" I gestured at the van, hopping as I waved.

Dave grinned, waved back, and kept driving to some other lucky winner's house. We watched until the van disappeared from sight. After I calmed down, I told Myra about the sweepstakes and the promise of riches to the recipient of the lucky winning number. You only had to return the entry form with the matching numbers to be set for life.

Myra sniffed and said, "Sounds like a waste of time and a stamp to me."

"You gotta have dreams, Myra," I maintained.

"Whatever." She gave me a sidewise gaze that said I had lost my mind. Myra can be too practical sometimes.

We picked up the open house signs, and dropped them at my car. I followed Myra to her spotless SUV, plucked a few flyers from my bag and handed them to her. She might know a buyer or two. We knew advertising the house in her neighborhood was a long shot. But the house could be an investment property for one of her wealthy neighbors—or a starter home for the offspring of the well-to-do. You never knew.

Back home, I heard the telephone ring as I unlocked the door. I rushed in, leaving the door ajar and dashed to the phone.

"Hello!?"

"I'm calling for Katelyn Baxter," a youthful sounding man said.

"This is she."

"Hi, we were at the showing for the house on Bluebird Street. My wife and I would like to make an offer."

"Excellent." I managed to keep my voice even, but couldn't hide a giddy tone as I responded. "I could meet you at the house to do the paperwork."

"About four thirty or five?" he offered.

"Perfect."

I had about an hour to get myself together, grab a quick bite, and present myself as a professional agent, and owner. It was a stretch. I'd need to be a quick study going through the forms the couple had to sign.

"You can do this," I repeated a mantra in front of the mirror, as I freshened my make-up and tamed my hair with spray. I grabbed my bag with the forms, adding a manila envelope and new file folder, all the while doing a happy dance.

Later, while I drove, I said a few prayers in homage to my *ad hoc* religious upbringing. Another disaster whose scars I bear. You don't want to know.

I tried Myra on my cell. It went to voicemail, "Hi, Myra. The couple from the open house this morning wants to make a bid. I'm on my way to Bluebird. We're going to meet between four thirty and five. If you can make it, great. Otherwise, I'll be talking to you."

The young couple was already there when I pulled up and parked in front of the house. They had apparently arranged childcare and were viewing the outside.

"We can get a puppy for the girls," the young woman said, enthused as she gazed into the chain-link, fenced backyard."

"There's a storage shed for the lawn mower," the young man added.

"We can have a garden," the woman said, a glow lighting up her face.

I was buoyed by the enthusiasm of the pair. They followed me to the door. Smiling, I opened the entry, and glanced over my shoulder at the two. "If your financing goes through, it sounds like you folks have a house."

The couple exchanged glances.

"Sure," the woman said. A tiny ping of doubt sounded in my consciousness. I squelched it, and let the couple in.

Inside, the man faced me, clearing his throat, "We aren't exactly prequalified."

"Okay. You need to find a lender. Usually, it's the bank you do business with," I said.

"Sure," he said. "We can do that."

"I gather this is your first home purchase?"

"Uh, yeah."

"And you have a job?"

"Oh, yeah. For sure."

I scrutinized the earnest young man and his wife. The gangly man had blemishes around his chin. The woman appeared more mature, but still very young.

"Do you mind if I ask how old you two are?" I asked, wincing.

"I am twenty-one years old." He drew himself to his full height, which I calculated just over a skinny six feet.

"I'm twenty-two. Mark married an older woman," his wife giggled.

"Cougar," he said, laughing.

"We met in high school. We worked at the local deli sandwich shop."

"Where do you work now?"

"Big Mart!" they said together.

"Okay." In the back of my mind with a sinking heart, I calculated what a couple with children and working at a discount store—even a major retailer, would have for an income. I struggled to keep an open mind. Being young, didn't make one irresponsible.

"Where do you live now?"

"We live with Mark's parents," the young woman responded.

"Oh," I brightened, thinking mom and dad could help them out.

"Yeah, they want us out because they're splitting up, and want to sell the house, so his dad can get his own digs."

What ever happened to happily ever after, and in sickness in health, I thought, sorting the forms, and marking the spaces for the pair to sign. *Yikes, this is getting messy.*

"But his mom is going to live with us. She wants to take care of the kids while we both work. Daycare is so expensive," she said, flipping back a stray lock of brown hair.

"It's always better to have family raise your children," I murmured, then mentally crossed my fingers, thinking about my chaotic childhood.

"I'm sure everything will work out for the best," I added, with a smile. I didn't believe it for a minute. "I think that will do, for now. You'll need to talk to a lender to find out if your income will qualify for a loan. Until then, I'll need earnest money to hold the house until you have a lender."

"How much?" the young man asked, uneasy.

"A thousand should do it," I said crisply. "When the loan goes through, the deposit is applied to the down payment and closing costs."

"I didn't bring my checkbook," he said, his thin face paling. "I didn't think you'd need money today."

"Earnest money means you are serious about the house." Sighing, I said, "Let's do this. I'll give you a copy of the paperwork today. Talk it over with your parents and any lender to see if your budget works with the home purchase. If it does, I'll need funds to keep the house off the market until closing. You can call and let me know. We can sign the documents and get your check at that time." It's always best to end on a high note.

"Uh, okay," he said, grinning.

"Until there's money down, the house stays on the market."

"Oh, the house is perfect!" the young wife said, grabbing the young man's hand.

"I'll wait for your call," I said, and shut the file folder.

"Can we see the house again?" the woman asked, her eyes on the man's face.

"Sure."

While the couple, holding hands, did one last walk-through of the home, I surveyed the kitchen. *Well, this is good practice. And, you never know,* I shrugged, *maybe the kids will come through. And, they hadn't mentioned karma.* I listened as the pair strolled through the rooms, their young voices high-pitched, excited about buying their first home.

My cell phone rang. It was Myra. "You got an offer—great!"

"Sort of—they're touring the house again. I gave them the paperwork, but they didn't put money down," I explained, my voice low, the couple approaching the kitchen where I waited.

"Uh, I don't like that," Myra said.

"Yeah." I sighed. "Me, neither. Oops got to go, I think they're ready to leave. Talk to you later."

The couple returned to the kitchen, their faces glowing with anticipation. The young man's arm circled the woman's shoulders. Her arm was wrapped around his waist as she rested her head against his shoulder. They gave each other a hug and a soulful glance before releasing their grasp on each other. The young man straightened and extended his hand. "We'll be in touch."

"I look forward to hearing from you," I replied, and shook his hand. I viewed the pair as they strolled out the front door, each deep in thought.

"Kids, they're just kids," I mused.

Summer was fading. Eddy was still in my spare bedroom. It was crunch time, and I needed a qualified buyer.

CHAPTER 25

Myra and I stepped up our open houses by adding Thursday afternoons to garner potential buyers. On this Thursday, a few lookers kept us busy until late afternoon.

Myra appeared chipper throughout the showing, while I was preoccupied with the uneasy reality that the house wasn't sold. The mystery of who'd left the bodies and how they were transported was solved. Paul Seever was dead. Michael Preston Ness and Mr. Randal were in custody. We had cleared the house of negativity. Now I was just worried because a buyer hadn't surfaced.

At the end of the open house while collecting brochures, I put aside my scenario of gloom and doom, and asked Myra, "How are you today?"

"Fantastic!"

"Great. What's going on?" I added the flyers to my bag.

"Remember my wreath bandit who morphed into a mail thief, who didn't warrant any police attention?" she appeared smug, adjusting her scarf.

"Yes?"

"The kid came to my house."

"No kidding?" I asked, dumbfounded, "What for?"

"To apologize."

"Really?!" I was impressed.

"Yes, he did. He came over, said he was sorry and brought a beautiful new wreath for the door. It has a fall motif with tans, deep reds, and browns that will complement my house," she said, satisfied.

"Terrific." I nodded, asking, "He decided a life of petty crime didn't pay?"

"It appears so," she grinned.

"What made him come around?"

"He had a little bit of help," she said with a chuckle.

"From your brother," I guessed.

"Uh huh, along with a little detecting from me."

"Really?"

"Remember, the police said I could ask the neighbors if they recognized the ne'er do well from the security photograph?"

"Yeah?"

"I looked up all the neighbors in our local residential directory. I chose families with kids about the same age as my thief and went on Facebook."

"You found him on Facebook? You're kidding!"

"I did," she smirked. "I matched my photograph with snapshots that he'd posted on his page, and gave everything to my brother."

"The police chief," I said with my eyebrow raised.

"Of course. He made a personal call to said neighbor. The next day the kid was at the door, red-faced, and apologetic. Both parents were watching to be sure he did the right thing," she said. "They were not happy with him."

"Great, Myra. I'm happy for you. You don't think he'll do it again?"

"No. I don't think so," she said, and she shook her head. "I think he's learned his lesson."

"Don't mess with Myra."

"You got it."

I surveyed my rehabbed house. I was glad Myra had caught her thief. But I couldn't stem my disappointment with the prospects from our open house. They were lookers, not buyers. A few were getting ideas for DIY projects.

I was getting panicky. The summer was winding down and my hopes were dwindling that the house would sell before school started. Families with children would want to have a home nailed down before the start of the school year. That left empty nesters or singles. Many of them would want maintenance free condos or townhouses.

I hadn't heard from my young couple. Truthfully, I knew it was for the best. I didn't want to sell to anyone who would have trouble making a mortgage.

But my home improvement demon was kicking in. I was itching for another project.

I had my eye on another house in the area that looked like it could use a little TLC. But I couldn't buy another property until I sold this one.

Discouraged, I glanced up from my guest list of potential buyers as Eddy sauntered in.

Myra glanced at Eddy and asked, "So I'll close up?" I nodded. She made quick business of gathering the rest of the sales brochures and business cards.

"Hi, Kate." He gazed around at the cozy ranch house. "Nice place. Hi, Myra." He added, "Bye, Myra," and winked with an irrepressible twinkle, as she headed to the door.

"Eddy." Myra nodded, grinning as she left, giving a quick wave.

"Thanks, Myra. I'll catch up later."

I faced Eddy. "It is a nice place." I didn't know why Eddy was using my name. I'd gotten so used to him calling me "Wifey." It sounded like my given name. "Do you want to buy it?"

"Let's get a drink and talk about it. Popov's?"

"Okay," I agreed. "You're buying," I added, and gave him a warning stare.

"Sure. I have a job now, Katelyn." He nodded, jovially.

"Okay." I was nonplussed. Maybe he could afford something. Then I gave myself a mental kick. This was Eddy, after all.

I did a quick walk through the house, switched off lights, and grabbed my purse while he waited outside for me.

"Let's take my car," I said, locking up.

"You're the boss," Eddy agreed.

I jumped in my Ford, while Eddy got in the passenger's side and adjusted the seat for his long legs. We headed to the restaurant.

Popov's was already crowded for the night's activities. There were singles unwinding, looking for a connection, and karaoke singers. We surveyed the room, and found a table on the fringe of the dance floor. I read the bar menu and checked my watch—too late for happy hour food, but not too late for happy hour wine.

I ordered chardonnay and Eddy ordered a beer. The waitress was new, a pretty blonde, and one I hadn't seen before. I made a point of tapping the menu where happy hour times were shown and ordered. After she left with our requests, we heard a tray of glassware hit the floor behind the bar.

We looked over to see the manager, the dark-haired woman known for her temper, chastising our waitress in broken English, "Missy, you break, you buy."

The young server flushed a bright red, but kept her tongue. She collected the broken serve ware while the older woman hovered, angry.

Embarrassed for the young woman, we looked away from the altercation and watched set-up for karaoke night. I don't know what possesses people to get up in front of other folks and sing. God bless them.

Need I say more? The couple of times I've seen a karaoke session, I've been the first to give the participants all the encouragement they deserve. I see karaoke as the poor man's answer to *The Voice*, *Idol* or any of the talent shows where the public and the audience weigh in on the merits of a performer.

In a softly lit bar, the aspiring singer can belt out a tune free of the judge's scathing reviews, and get polite applause for a rendition of any tune from the forgiving, and likely alcohol-impaired, audience.

Eddy had a decent voice. He could carry a tune, and true to his nature, loved the attention of the patrons and any unattached women. After he sang, "You're Going to Miss Me When I'm Gone," to the crowd, flushed by the applause, he sat back at our table.

We got to the business at hand.

"Are you serious about buying the house?"

"I can't sleep in your spare room forever."

"Good point," I conceded. "Lending practices have tightened up, Eddy. Two years of gainful employment history, and twenty, maybe thirty percent down. No messy marital status. Married or single, no separated. Divorced. Period."

"How much is the house?"

I told Eddy the price of the nicely redone home; he said, "Seems reasonable."

"It is. Reasonable."

"Okay. I don't have two years' steady employment. And, I haven't got thirty, or even twenty percent for a down payment. My divorce from Lola isn't final," he added sheepishly.

"Uh huh. How about rent to own?" *It would be nice to have my home back.* "For two years. Until your employment history is solid, and you qualify for a bank loan."

"That might work," he said and grinned.

"Okay. I'll draw up the paperwork."

"How about we toast to it?" Eddy asked, his smile wide and possibly amorous. I ignored any suggestion and held up my wine glass. He held up his beer and I clicked the wine glass against his bottle.

"Here's to your new home." I laughed, relieved my house would have an occupant that could provide income. "Tomorrow, I'll get the paperwork together, and we'll have it signed and notarized."

"You're one tough cookie," he grumbled, still smiling.

I shrugged. I figured I owed Eddy a break after he took one to the groin wrestling Mr. Randal in my living room. Just not a free ride.

He threw down money to pay our tab. Our waitress took Eddy's bills, and he got up after she returned with change.

"Let's go," he swallowed the remainder of his beer. I rose, and followed him. As we left, the waitress went behind the bar, tugged off her apron and threw it at the woman who reprimanded her. "I quit," she huffed, and grabbed her bag from under the bar, flinging the straps over her shoulder.

Good for her; she has courage. Unfortunately, Popov's had lost another employee.

At least she waited until after she'd collected our bill and charged happy hour prices. It was the recession. Everyone was tense, stretching every dollar to make a living. Myself included.

In silence, I drove to the Bluebird Street house where Eddy had left his truck. He unfolded his legs, and gave my knee a squeeze. "See ya back at the ranch." He got out and sauntered to his truck. Another reason I had a soft spot for Eddy. Despite his failings, he was good-natured, and still pretty cute.

When he got in, I was camped out on the sofa with Boots. He headed to the second bedroom he had dutifully put together. I was a little unnerved by Eddy renting my renovated house and decided to stay up and tell Boots about the whole thing. Get another male's opinion. Before long, Eddy's snores echoed through the bedroom and filtered into the living room.

I readied the paperwork for Eddy the next day. Then, carried Boots into the master bedroom. After a couple of hours, tossing and turning, I finally crashed.

"Dang it!" I woke in a panic and scrambled out of bed. It was my market research day. I had an uneasy truce with Jennifer. It was iffy I'd ever hear from the wine distributor. Until Eddy was paying rent on the Bluebird house, my finances were thin. I dashed to the kitchen to make coffee, and showered while it brewed. Between sips of java, I dressed, threw on makeup, got kibble for Boots, then dashed out the door.

"Double dang!" Cursing the noisy engine, I fired up the wagon. I backed out of the garage and pulled onto the street. A black car slithered from a side street and darted in behind my car. Checking the rearview mirror, my jaw dropped. Jackson Randal was behind the wheel of the hearse, his front bumper inches from my rear. My only choice was to drive straight ahead. I sped up, he sped up. I slowed, he slowed. All the while, he glared, his eyes nearly black, through his windshield, somber and hateful.

"You're supposed to be in jail, Mr. Randal," I muttered. I made a quick right at a stop light, trying to lose the hearse. He followed, tapping the Escort's bumper with the front of his car. My neck jerked, and the back of my head smacked against the headrest.

"Ouch! That hurts, you bastard." Inhaling, I punched the gas pedal to the floor, gunning the engine. The wagon lurched ahead and I raced to the police precinct station which I gauged was within ten blocks of Randal's collision with my bumper.

"Leave me alone!" I yelled, and blasted my horn.

I poured on the gas, pulling around a bicyclist, my heart pounding, narrowly missing the male cyclist, probably a student from the backpack he toted. "Hey!" he shouted and gave me an angry hand signal.

The commotion didn't faze Randal as he drag-raced the hearse. He forced the biker to the sidewalk from the bike lane. I sped up. The sound of car repairs I'd ignored for the past few months got louder. There was a resounding screech and bang from under the hood of the wagon. The car slowed and came to a stop. Panicked, I pumped the gas. Nothing.

I looked out the driver's side window squarely into the sneering face of Jackson Randal in the driver's seat of his hearse. His car blocked my door. He reached over for an object on his passenger's seat, and lifted his arm. I caught an image of a black handgun before I ducked, throwing myself to the passenger's side. Jamming both feet against the driver's door, I clutched the passenger's side door handle, twisted, and rolled out.

"Damn!" I hit the sidewalk, my right shoulder and ribs screamed with pain. I bounded up and ran, "He's trying to kill me! He's got a gun!"

The bicyclist who was forced to the sidewalk pedaled behind me. He made a U-turn and biked off in the opposite direction. Catching my breath, I kept running, my lungs aching. The best I could hope was that the cyclist had a cell phone and would call the police, or another motorist would alert the cops.

I heard the sound of tires on the road beside me. Glancing over my shoulder, I saw Randal's hearse jump onto the sidewalk, right front bumper pointed straight for me. Leaping, I landed in the grass beyond the sidewalk.

Randal jerked the car to the left, gun in his right hand, "You bitch!" he screamed as the car fishtailed and crashed into a power pole. Broken pieces of the hearse flew, scattering wreckage on the street and walkway.

His windshield shattered and Randal's head bounced against the steering wheel with the force of the impact. The hearse stopped and he slumped over the wheel, horn blaring as the engine whined.

Sirens screamed and two squad cars arrived, one parked in front of the hearse, the other behind. The police officers jumped out and ran to the car. There was an odor of fuel in the air. Gasoline leaked from the car and ran down the street in a small stream.

"Stand back!" one officer yelled, and the police backed away from the hearse.

KABOOM!! The gasoline ignited in an explosion of smoky black, orange, and red, with Randal at the wheel. That was the last thing I saw.

CHAPTER 26

I woke in the emergency room of the County hospital. Thankfully, it wasn't the hospital I'd worked for, and where Michael Preston Ness had done his walk of shame.

Myra sat in a chair next to my bed. "You had quite a morning. How do you feel?"

"I ache all over." With a moan, I rubbed my head. "What happened?"

"You don't remember?"

"The last thing I remember is an explosion. I was running," I said, and felt my forehead.

"Yes, you were," Myra confirmed.

"Jackson Randal was trying to run you over, like he did Jimmy Woo," Sheriff Don said, standing by the door.

"Yee gads; now I remember." I felt my neck. "How did I get here?"

"His car blew up when he hit the power pole," the sheriff said.

"You were knocked out from the force of the explosion," Myra added.

"Jackson Randal was Jimmy's drug dealer?" I asked, massaging a dull throb at my temple. "I thought Randal was in jail?"

"He made bail, and came straight for you," Sheriff Don said, adding, "with a vengeance."

"Terrific," I said, groaning.

Sheriff Don paused; his face somber. "Remember, I said there could be something more behind Jackson Randal leaving bodies at foreclosed houses?"

"What?"

"Randal was a body broker."

"A what?" Myra asked.

"A body broker. He ran a company out of the funeral home that advertised it could find bodies, store, and process body parts. He advertised online."

"But selling body parts is illegal, isn't it?" I asked.

"He didn't exactly sell the parts," the sheriff paused. "It's an industry that is paid to find the bodies, store, and process. He harvested bones, joints, and tissues from bodies. He was paid for the services, not the actual part.

"Yikes, isn't that skirting the law?" Myra asked.

"It's legal, just not well regulated," Sheriff Don said.

"If it's legal, and he made money, why did he leave the bodies in foreclosed houses?" I asked. I rubbed my forehead, trying to concentrate.

"That's where it got sticky. Randal's refrigeration unit was broken, along with the crematorium. His plan was to store the body temporarily in an unoccupied house, crank up the air conditioning, then retrieve it later. He was banking on the recession, and that foreclosed houses wouldn't sell as fast as they did," he said. "He always meant to come back for the bodies."

"He got the bodies from Michael Preston Ness, and double payment for services from the county because of their convoluted accounting system," I surmised, running the scheme through my mind. "But, don't people have to be donors?" I asked, with a frown.

"It's called whole body donation, different deal. Ness forged the paperwork for charity cases for whole body donations at the hospital. That got the ball rolling for the body to go to Randal for storage and processing."

"Donating an organ is different from donating a body?" Myra asked.

"Yep. Like I said, not a whole lot of regulation. Once the body is processed for bones, joints, and tissues—anything salable—the remains are cremated."

"OMG. His crematorium was broken, so he buried the remainder on the land?" I ventured a guess, groaning. Recalling my visit to the funeral home and the woods that bordered the business.

"Yep. He was trying to disguise the fact by clearing the land—burning what he could in the dead of night, using wood piles as camouflage."

"How could he get away with that?" I sat up and faced the sheriff.

"He didn't. Used baking soda and vinegar to hide the smell. But people got suspicious. A couple of residents complained about fires and unusual activity in the wee hours of the morning."

"Terrible," Myra said. "Those poor people. Randal made money from their deaths. What did he do with all the money?"

"He gambled it away. Owed money all over town, even to the Russian mob," the sheriff said.

"Not Popov's? Not Ivan and Maggie!" Myra and I viewed the sheriff, alarmed. I remembered rumors about the restaurant being a hub for illegal activities.

"Different Russians," the sheriff said, and gave a small smile.

"Thank goodness!" Myra and I said together.

"Randal's actions were horrific," I said. I gingerly touched a bruise on my temple.

"Yep. We couldn't keep him in jail because we hadn't found anything. Investigators sent in a cadaver dog and the animal hit on human remains. They're searching the lot as we speak. But we do have Jackie Randal in custody."

"Who?" I asked, flexing my hands.

"Jackie is Jackson Randal's daughter."

"Oh?" I shrugged.

"She scouted vacant houses for Jackson and Paul Seever to leave the bodies."

"Okay." I massaged my shoulder, shaking my head.

"You would know her if you saw her. Got blue hair, styled kind of spiky. Has an eyebrow piercing?" the sheriff added.

"That woman!" I sat up again, groaned, and laid back. "She's Jackson Randal's daughter?"

"The very one," Sheriff Don said.

"The young woman from the first open house?" Myra asked. "Who accused you of leaving Jimmy's body there?"

"Yep. It's an old tactic—a good defense is a good offense," Sheriff Don said, with a wry smile.

"I'll be darned," Myra said. "She accused you, when she was part of the scheme."

"Yep, she sure did," I said, weary.

"We picked her up when the owner of Grape Vines complained about vandalism. Got her place of employment, Randal's Reswell Funeral Home. Put two and two together, and she cracked under questioning," the sheriff said, satisfied.

"Yep, that's her all right." I remembered the mess of the wine display. "Doug must have been calling the police when I left."

"What?" Myra asked.

"Long story." I moaned, feeling another stab of pain from my shoulder.

"Awful, making his own daughter part of his trickery," Myra said, shaking her head.

"Yikes," I said, feeling my noggin, and flexing my arms and legs. I hurt all over.

"You'll want to go slowly," Myra admonished. "You have a small lump on your head and you are going to be sore. But nothing is broken. They'll keep you overnight for observation."

"What happened to my car?" I asked, wincing.

"The engine blew. The car had a good life, a long life," Myra said, smiling.

"Terrific."

"I'll loan you mine," she said. "I'm in the market."

"I can't do that, Myra. You know my rule."

"No arguments. Rules are meant to be broken. You need to get some rest now."

A nurse appeared to usher Myra and the sheriff out. Myra left first.

"We'll talk more at the station, Kate," Sheriff Williams said, as he left, his voice low and reassuring. "I'm glad you're okay."

He still has that air of masculinity and warmth going on. I closed my eyes, and passed out.

CHAPTER 27

I went home the next morning, no worse for the trauma.

It's thought to be good luck if it rains while the sun shines. Light rain streaked against a sunny sky while I helped Eddy move into the Bluebird Street house the next day. It was bittersweet. I was glad the house was occupied and I'd have a steady income until Eddy could buy it, or it sold. I added a provision to the lease that said he'd vacate the premises if I found a buyer.

"Whatever you want, Katie." Eddy, as always, was amenable. We both knew it would have to be a super sweet deal to enforce the clause. We had history, after all.

I kind of missed him calling me, 'Wifey,' and we couldn't rekindle what we had early in our lives. But you have to let go of some dreams.

Lola let Eddy take the rest of his stuff from the apartment they'd shared. I wasn't surprised she'd hung on to it. Eddy had a way with women. No matter how poorly he'd treated a woman, they always forgave him. He filled his pickup and I met him at the house to help him get settled.

I left Eddy while he unpacked to the sounds of the radio blaring country tunes. I drove to my townhouse in style—Myra's SUV. It drove like a dream, no noisy engine, comfy seat, great floor mats. Life was good.

I pulled into the driveway and parked in the garage. Wayne and Mrs. Gilman were planting another new shrub next to her patio area. Mrs. Gilman steadied the top of the plant. Wayne, his silver hair braided, shoveled dirt around the base of the bush.

"I can add in tulip and daffodil bulbs for spring color," Mrs. Gilman said, as Wayne finished packing the dirt. "It will look wonderful." She sounded thrilled with the new plant, her face aglow. She wore Kelly-green colored hoodie and sweatpants.

"That sounds great, Gillie," Wayne agreed jovially, pausing to wipe a bead of perspiration from his forehead. "I'll make a new planter for the patio this winter."

"Oh, Wayne. A plant-holder sounds lovely. Something in red cedar?"

"Consider it done." Wayne pressed the mound of dirt with the shovel. He was brushing off his faded jeans when I met up with the pair.

"Katelyn," Mrs. Gilman, acknowledged, patting her tousled hair.

"Hello, kiddo!" Wayne chortled. "Glad to see you in one piece." He hugged me.

"You had quite a scare," Mrs. Gilman added. "Myra told us all about it."

"Yep. But it's done now." I wanted to put the whole ugly business of Randal's chase and the accident behind me. Not to mention, his side business.

"What's going on?" I admired the new plant, a Rhododendron with thick waxy foliage.

"Will ya look at this? I tell ya, Gillie is a genius with flowers and shrubs. This is going to make this place first rate."

"Oh, Wayne," Mrs. Gilman protested with a shy smile, blushing a bright pink.

"Very nice," I agreed.

"So, that Eddy of yours is moving out," Wayne said, as he dug in his front shirt pocket for a pack of unfiltered Camel's.

"Yep. He's going to rent the Bluebird Street house. It'll be an income. Pay for the house, at least until I get a buyer."

Mrs. Gilman continued to admire her new plant.

"Bet ya kind of got used to the company," Wayne added. I was never any good at hiding my feelings. I had one of those faces which showed every emotion, and I hated it. Suddenly, I felt myself misting up.

"Sure. But it's time he got back on his feet." Abruptly, I added, "Well, guys, have fun. I've got to feed Boots." I wanted the safety of my home before I made a fool of myself in front of the seniors. At the moment, it appeared love was in the air for everyone except for yours truly. I knew it was best Eddy moved out, but wasn't prepared for my reaction. *He'll be back, like a bad dream.*

I squared my shoulders, head high, as I rounded the end of the townhouses to the front entrance. As I was about to open the main door, the sheriff's car drove up and parked in the driveway. The bubble light wasn't lit, and the siren was off. That was a plus.

Sheriff Don switched off the engine and got out. I halted and wondered, what trouble I might have gotten myself into this time?

"Hello Kate," the Sheriff said, his blue eyes twinkling, as he walked towards me.

"Sheriff, what can I do for you?" I asked, my mind searching for loose ends on Ariel's death, or any more bodies left by Paul Seever and the funeral director. I got nothing.

"This is purely a social call, Kate," the sheriff said. He smiled and the lines at the edge of his eyes crinkled, "Call me Don."

"In that case, come in." I pivoted and he followed me through the corridor of the complex.

I unlocked the house door, threw my handbag on a kitchen chair, and draped my jacket over the back. "Please, have a seat. Coffee?" My heart skipped a beat, as I tried to appear casual and composed.

"I'd like that."

I put on the coffee, and faced the sheriff, surveying his strong jaw and silver-touched blond hair. He was comfortably settled at the table where Boots sniffed at his feet.

"I have tickets to the Policeman's Holiday Dance. All proceeds go to the widows and orphans fund; can I put you down for a ticket?"

My stomach dropped, and I kept a note of disappointment out of my voice. "Sure," I said, and went for my purse. As I dug around in the handbag, he added, "And I would be honored, if I could have the pleasure of your company for the dance?"

"Are you asking me out, Sheriff?" My stomach did a flip.

"Yes, Kate, I'm asking you out." He cleared his throat, his deep blue eyes focused on mine.

"I'd love to." My mind was whirling.

"It's a date," he said, with a broad smile. I offered my hand for a shake to seal the date. He took my hand in his, his fingers stroking the top, holding my hand in his for a long minute.

The coffeemaker gave a gurgle and a hiss, which meant it had finished perking. I withdrew my hand, "Cream or sugar?"

"Black." A man who understood coffee. I filled two mugs and joined him at the table.

"Sheriff, I have a question about Mr. Randal." The thought had nagged at me even though the case was closed.

"It's Don, please. What's on your mind?"

"Okay," I paused, and asked, "Don. How did he get Jimmy Woo's body in the attic?"

"Randal was a low-tech kind of guy. He had a two-wheeler to move the body. Used bungee cords to secure the body to the cart, undid the body from the cart, secured the body to a rope. Threw the rope over the attic beams. The rope acted as a pulley to hoist the weight through the access panel. With Jimmy being a small man and with both men, Paul Seever and Jackson Randal moving the body, it was doable." He took a gulp of coffee.

"Why the attic?" I sipped my coffee. "Was he coming back for him?"

"Okay, that's three questions, Kate," he grinned. "Don't really know. Can't ask Randal or Seever, they're both dead. Might be Jimmy's death was personal. He owed Randal for drugs; that's why Randal killed him. Don't know what plans he had for his body."

"Thank goodness, he was found out," and I gave a shudder.

"Yep. Sad state of affairs."

"I guess that does it," I said, sitting back. Sheriff Don took a gulp, finished his coffee and stood up, "I'll be going. Glad you weren't hurt in the chase, Kate."

"Me, too."

The air in the room got very warm. Don leaned down and kissed me gently on the lips. The feel of his soft mouth on mine left me speechless. Then, he went to the door and let himself out.

CHAPTER 28

Ariel's townhouse went into foreclosure. There was a sign the lender would be showing it the next day. I knew I couldn't swing a deal, but couldn't get it out of my mind. I was obsessed. I had to see what the bank wanted for it.

As soon as the unit opened for showing, I went in.

"Hi." The representative from the bank was a cheerful petite, blonde woman who stood eager to greet us at the kitchen counter. "Please sign in. Feel free to look around and ask questions."

"Thanks." I didn't see any reason to say I lived down the hall. I signed the guest list and took the spec sheet from the table. The floor plan was the same as the other homes. The price was less than what I'd paid for my unit.

"This is a great deal!" The figure made me a little giddy.

"It is, isn't it? She smiled. "I'm showing it as a favor to the bank. You can talk to this fellow," and she handed me a card, "about financing."

Wayne sauntered in about that time. "Thought I heard your voice, kiddo. Looking to buy another house?"

"Hi, Wayne."

"I live in the first unit," I said, fessing up.

She watched us; her curiosity raised. "So, you both know about the … incident?"

"Boy, do we," I said, and rolled my eyes.

"Yep," he said, and chuckled, brushing his hair behind his ears.

"The price reflects the, ah … negative effect the unfortunate incident may have had on the value of the townhouse," she said. "And, of course, any updating the unit needs."

"Updating, as in changing the ghastly paint color," I said, surveying the walls. I was already thinking about it. A coat of primer, couple coats of a nice, neutral color.

"Yeah, there's a lot of purple. Purple haze," he said, snickering.

"Of course, colors are a personal choice," the agent offered.

"The carpet needs to be replaced. It's worn," I said. "And, you never know how well it dried after the soaking it got." Mindful of the night we trekked through the unit to Ariel's bathroom.

"Yeah, probably best. Carpeting is easy enough," Wayne agreed.

"And, new appliances are in order. It doesn't appear as if Ariel did much in the way of cleaning." The stove burners had baked on food. Mentally, I tallied the cost of a new dishwasher, refrigerator, and range.

I went into the second bedroom, then entered the master bedroom. Wayne followed.

Both were empty. With Ariel's furniture and personal belongings gone, there was a neglected air to the townhouse.

We stopped short in the master bathroom. "Should be gutted," Wayne said.

"Yep," I nodded. "What do you think it would run?"

"Wouldn't be too bad," he replied, and threw out a figure. "I have some contacts with plumbing supply houses."

"Gee, I don't know, Wayne. I don't think I can get financing. And," I added, wincing, "do you think I could sell a home where someone died tragically?"

"You know, kiddo, people die all the time. Now, it's a shame about Ariel. But, who better to rehab this unit, if not you? We've all got homes in this development. If we don't get this unit rehabbed and sold, it's gonna take down everybody's housing value."

I knew Wayne was challenging me. He had a valid point. I couldn't dwell on the negative. We had to dispel the bad energy and move on.

"Could Myra swing something with the bank? She could be part-owner or something?" Wayne asked. My natural aversion to having friends help with any financial situation reared its head.

"No, Myra wouldn't want a financial interest in rehabbing property." She was already lending me her slick SUV. Then thinking aloud, I added, "But, maybe she would help in another way."

We headed to the kitchen where the agent waited. She was fiddling with her cell phone.

An idea brewed in my mind. "Does Ariel Kominski's family know of her illegal use of marijuana and other additives?" I asked the chirpy blonde.

The woman's eyes widened in panic, and she responded, "I'm not privy to that information. I'm sure the family would want to stay out of any controversy."

"I'm sure they would," I agreed, nodding sympathetically.

It struck me as odd that Ariel's wealthy family would let her townhouse go into bankruptcy, and they wouldn't do better by one of their own. After all, if Ariel had been my daughter or sister, I wouldn't want her memory tarnished. Or my financial investment in another business—say the Komin's Food Stores—tarnished.

When we left the showing, the agent was busy shuffling papers, avoiding eye contact with either of us. There were two hours remaining on the open house.

"I'll run the figures on what it would cost to rehab the unit," Wayne promised, as we parted ways and went to our respective homes.

"It couldn't hurt," I said, shrugging. Not sure if what I had in mind would fly.

I had a heart-to-heart with Myra over the telephone about Ariel's townhouse unit.

"Let me see if my brother can talk to the lender," Myra said. "Maybe the bank can talk to the family. Sometimes the best way to get things done is to approach it from a different angle."

"Okay, you go, girl. Let me know what's going on." I brewed a fresh pot of coffee, and took my cup to the patio table where I sat and listened to the sounds of birds chirping, and watched gray squirrels scurrying about. I didn't have long to wait.

I heard the distant sound of a telephone ringing in Ariel's unit. Muffled voices after that. Ariel's patio door slammed. Still straining to listen, I got up and headed to the front of the townhomes. The representative from

Ariel's bank collected her sign, tossed it in the trunk of her car, got in, and drove off.

My cell phone rang, and I jumped, quickly answering.

"It's a done deal," Myra said, and chortled. "My brother called the banker. The banker called the family. They called the family lawyer. The lawyer advised the family to buy the unit to avoid any negative publicity. Which, they agreed to."

"Okay. That will leave the unit vacant and in need of rehabbing."

"The attorney will draw up an agreement to have the unit renovated and donated to a charitable foundation. The enterprise will be run by the Kominski family and dedicated in Ariel's memory."

"Who was the unfortunate victim of Paul Seever and drug use?" I added.

"You got it."

"Did your brother, during his investigation, ever find out what Paul and Ariel were going to celebrate the night Ariel was killed?"

"You know, I asked him that question. He said Ariel's family was about to put her back in the will. She would inherit a fortune when either of her parents died. They had cut her out of the estate when she got into trouble with drugs. She convinced them she was clean."

"Which she wasn't."

"No. But, we think she was going to tell Paul he could stop worrying about money. Her family was taking her back into the fold—and the will."

"So, I wonder what happened?"

"Paul had been using. Maybe it was the marijuana mixture. Who knows? He could have had hallucinations. For all we know, he could have seen Ariel holding the hairdryer and thought it was a weapon when he strangled her."

"Yikes. He did have a strange air about him that night," I recalled. "Wayne called him creepy."

"Oh," Myra added, "part of the deal asks for a garden on the grounds to be established in Ariel's memory."

"I have just the person to do a garden."

"Good. My brother will suggest you as a Rehab Specialist."

"Perfect, Myra, I appreciate it."

The Kominski family lawyer called the next morning, and stopped by with a contract from the family with a figure for renovating Ariel's unit and establishing a garden plot in her memory. It outlined the expectations for renovation, along with a generous sum for the project manager, yours truly. The figure took my breath away, and I lost no time calling Jennifer at the research company.

I hummed a little of Johnny Paycheck's tune, "Take This Job and Shove It!" while I dialed the research group. Jennifer took it in stride. "If you ever want to pursue opportunities as a market research professional again," she trilled, "call me."

"Thanks, Jennifer, I will," I promised, with my fingers crossed and an eye roll. The study on hemorrhoids had been the pits. With Eddy renting my house and a generous sum to rehab Ariel's unit, I figured

I'd do okay for the immediate future.

Wayne and I went to work on Ariel's place. For a full month, we worked at a feverish pace to repaint, gut the bathroom, replace carpets, and install new appliances. Finished, we stood back, awed at the transformation.

"It looks bright, shiny new," I said, reveling in the change.

"It sure does," Wayne agreed. He was covered in dust and construction grime, and I was in grungy work garb.

"So, you and Gillie are on for this evening?" I had started calling Mrs. Gilman, Gillie, because Wayne did, and because the seniors appeared to spend most evenings with each other. I observed their blossoming relationship through a thick veil of envy and embarrassment.

"Yep, wouldn't miss it for anything," he chortled.

"Good."

I brushed my hair away from my face, and wiped the sweat off my forehead with the back of my hand. Grabbing my mug of coffee, I waited as Wayne took one last glance, and we let ourselves out of the newly refurbished unit.

"Seven o'clock," I said.

"Seven, it is."

I showered and dressed in black jeans and black blouse. It seemed appropriate for the evening's activities. I shrugged at my mass of curls and blasted my hair with gel spray, another new goo. I grabbed Boots and tucked him under my arm.

It was precisely seven o'clock when I met Wayne and Gillie outside of the redone unit. Wayne had graciously picked up the fellow I'd coined "broccoli man" from the neighborhood. He was cleaned up and wore a new plaid shirt with red suspenders and new blue jeans. Bob, broccoli man's real name, appeared nervous with his wispy hair combed back and tucked behind his ears.

Tension filled the air while I opened the unit. Myra joined our group toting a picnic basket. Her nails were done and her hair fresh from the salon. She wore a jacket, slacks, silk blouse, scarf, and carried a designer handbag. Her attitude resigned, she tossed me a wry smile and deposited the basket on the new granite countertop. She opened the carrier, and removed bottles of wine, one white and one red, crystal glasses and a lavender scented candle. She did an eye roll, and took out a bundle of sage and a plate for the cleansing ritual.

She lit the candle, and poured the wine. Each of us accepted a glass. Standing in a circle, we clicked our glasses together in a toast, chanting, "to new beginnings."

I put my glass on the counter, lit the sage bundle, and held it up. We passed the dish to each other and let the smoke waft over our bodies. I carried the dish with the lit sage through the unit. Silently, I said *thank you* to the gods of good fortune as I strolled through the townhouse. Everyone followed in single file as we made our way through the bedrooms, then to the bathroom.

Stopping outside the master bath, pausing to gaze at the fresh master bedroom, I let the smoke from the sage permeate the room.

"Schreeeeeeeeech!" The smoke alarm pierced the silence and I gasped.

"Oh, my!" Gillie was the first to talk.

"Open the windows!" Wayne yelled over the din, and he went to unlatch the patio slider. Bob followed, waving the smoke out of the room.

I blew out the sage packet, put it on the counter and joined everyone in wild gesturing. We pushed the smoke out of the townhome through the open slider and windows.

The shrill noise mercifully stopped. Everyone laughed nervously, nerves on edge.

I gazed at Myra. She groaned, took a large swallow of wine and said, "Not again!"

CHAPTER 29

"Do you think cops get all dressed up for this thing?" I asked, exasperated as Myra inspected my outfit. It was a sleeveless, slinky, black, knee-length cocktail dress. I felt awkward out of my jeans and sweatshirt, not to mention wearing high heels.

We were in my living room while Myra observed my walk, or attempt to walk. She was trying to whip me into shape for the Policeman's Holiday Dance. I was a tough subject.

"This is an outfit that will go anywhere," she insisted. "If the other women or officers are in casual attire, you slip on strappy low heels. This little bolero sweater minimizes the "hot" factor. If not, go for the full throttle style with the heels and skip the sweater."

"But, how will I know before we get there?" I whined, smoothing the dress.

"You'll know when the sheriff picks you up."

"How?"

"By the way he looks at you in the dress, silly goose."

I examined myself in the full-length mirror with the "full throttle" mode, turning every which way. I looked good. Myra had insisted I go to her hair stylist to mold my hair into a semblance of hairstyle, rather than let it do its usual wild, curly do.

We'd spent the morning at her hairdresser's and had lunch at a very nice little cafe. She was happy to give me the full princess routine and I could get used to being pampered.

"Okay, now try it dressed down," Myra said.

"You are kind of pushy, you know." Gratefully, I slipped out of the heels. Then, I put on the low, black, strappy shoes and sweater.

"I see what you mean." The effect was still striking, but not overwhelming. "I should go with this. It would be more me. Besides, I'm not sure where the sheriff's head is at. He probably wants to take someone safe, not a bombshell."

"Okay, you can let him decide," Myra said. "But, based on what my brother said, people go all out for this event. It's the social event of the year. Some of the men even wear tuxes."

"Great," I groaned. "I'll be underdressed."

"It's always better to be underdressed, rather than overdressed for a special occasion."

Of course, it's best to dress appropriately," she said, her eyebrows raised for emphasis.

"Oh, all right." I removed the sweater, and slipped back into the killer high heels.

"Excellent," Myra said, decisively. "He can always tell you if it's over the top."

"Yeah, like men are good judges of what's too much."

"You've got that right," she agreed, and laughed. "I'll let you relax before your big night. Let me know how it goes. I have to run."

"Thanks for everything, Myra. You've been a rock through it all. The car, the bodies, the Bluebird house. Now this." I hugged her.

"Nonsense. It's perfectly fine. That's what friends are for." She stepped back, sniffed, and brushed a stray lock of hair from her face.

"If it's a dud of an evening, it won't be because of you."

"You'll do fine. Any man would be lucky to be with you."

"Myra, you're the best."

After she left, I practiced walking in the heels. I traded low heels for high heels, sweater off, sweater on. I futzed with my hair, trying to keep in in place. It was perfect and I wanted to be at my best for the sheriff and our night out.

My doorbell rang a few minutes before seven. I opened the door and held my breath at the sight of a man I'd never seen before. The sheriff was dressed in a dark gray suit with a gray shirt and maroon colored tie. His broad shoulders filled out his suit coat, and I caught the faint scent of aftershave. His hair was brushed to a sheen; his face was tan, and his deep blue eyes lit up when he saw me.

"Hi," I said, feeling a blush warm my face.

"Hi, yourself."

We stood, face to face, for an awkward moment.

"Can I come in?" He broke the silence first.

"Oh sure," I stammered, and stood aside to let him in. I stepped past him and shut the door. At the same moment, my ankle wobbled in my heels and I tumbled into him. He caught me, and I felt his strength, his breath against my neck. His breath had a minty smell, mingled with the scent of his cologne.

Instinctively, my face tilted towards his. With a sparkle in his eyes, his lips lightly brushed my lips.

"Meow." Boots was at my feet and rubbing against my legs.

"Sorry, Sheriff," I muttered, gaining my balance, and running my hands along my hips.

"I'm not," he said, his voice low, while his hand cupped my chin. "Drop the sheriff. Call me Don." He drew me into his arms. Intuitively, I leaned my head back and he kissed my lips long and deep, until my toes curled in my shoes.

There was a sharp knock at the door. My eyes flew open, and I jumped away from Don's embrace. He dropped his arms and stepped back. I gasped, startled.

"Wifey?" Eddy's voice came. "Hey, are you in there?"

THE END

KATELYN'S HOME IMPROVEMENT TIPS

- If a small portion of paint is needed for a closet, or small area, I'll mix leftover neutral colors from different projects. It's probably best not to mix different sheens, i.e., satin, and flat, but it's doable.

- The scent of cigarette smoke is tough to remove from a car. Dust the inside with baking soda and leave for a couple of days, or leave an open box in the car. Try leaving coffee beans in the vehicle if you like the smell of coffee. They will neutralize the odor. Clean hard surfaces with vinegar, and shampoo upholstery and carpet.

- Buy the best quality paint you can afford. It goes on smoother with fewer drips and covers flaws better. Cleans up easier, too.

- Curb appeal lures a potential buyer into a house. Fresh paint on the door, hardware, new home numerals, and flowers all encourage people to buy. Crime scene tape, not so much.

- Skills like carpentry and drywall are best left to the professionals. Better to find a skilled tradesperson, rather than DIY. It's less frustrating and less costly in the end.

- Whenever I get a bug for frugal living, I go on the Internet for ideas. I've gotten recipes for homemade laundry soap and powder dishwasher detergent, and tried both with varied success.

- Furnishing a home with furniture and accessories will help sell a home. If staging a vacant house isn't in the budget, a clean house always sells faster than one that needs a scrubbing.

• To rid a basement of a musty smell, put out jars of white vinegar. It takes a few days, but clears up the odor—now you have to figure out what caused the stale air.

• To rid aphids from flowers, mix a small quantity of dishwashing soap in a bucket of water and douse the plants. It's a natural and inexpensive method to rid the plants of pests.

• Check smoke detectors regularly to ensure they are in working order. There is an aerosol spray available at home stores for the purpose. You can check smoke detectors with the real thing, matches and smoke, but use caution.

• A combination of two cups water, one tablespoon white vinegar, one teaspoon of baking soda and a dozen drops of essentials oils will make a spray deodorizer for household smells. Soak a hand towel with white vinegar and wave it throughout the house to rid cigarette smoke smells.

• Give the bathtub due respect by installing a hairdryer housing compartment a safe distance from running water.

• Yep, you guessed it. Dollar for dollar, insulating a home can save bunches on heating and cooling bills, not to mention cut unwanted sound travel.

• Any stain is tough. If you have a wine spill, the best time to remove is before it dries. Blot the stain first. Depending on the area, try white wine or club soda. Soak fabric with equal mix of Dawn dishwashing soap and hydrogen peroxide, and clean. The best thing to do is drink all the wine, thereby avoiding any unfortunate stains.

• Painting into a corner with one color and using another color on adjacent walls with leftover paint is one way to stretch paint and avoid a trip to the store.

• The factory codes you get when you purchase a garage door opener should always be changed. It is possible someone could have the same code to open your garage—and your house, if the garage connects to the house.

• For added home security with a sliding patio door, use an old broom handle (sans broom section) in the track section when the slider is closed. It doesn't have to be pretty, just functional. I'm all for pretty and functional though.

• There are bars designed to slip under a doorknob and prop from the floor for security. If you need something in a hurry, shove a chair back under the doorknob to prevent an intruder. Simple security measures, like locking your doors and windows while at home are a good idea. It may not stop an intruder, but will slow them down.

• Clean the tracks of a sliding glass patio door with a rag and alcohol. Lubricate with oil to keep the door in smooth working order.

• In my humble opinion; the best home is a mortgage-free home. After your monthly payment, make a separate payment each month towards the principal portion of the mortgage. It saves a bundle on interest and cuts the length of the loan, and you won't even miss the money.

• Once your home is paid for, put a set sum in a separate bank account, much like a mortgage payment. It's money for taxes, insurance, and maintenance. It works for cars and repairs, as well.

• It is possible to dry out carpet. It's important to work quickly as mold can grow. Remove water, use fans to dry carpet and a dehumidifier to remove moisture. Clean and sanitize carpet. Clean walls and floor moldings.

• My final tip is an adage from Pliny, a Roman philosopher, "Home is where the heart is." Make your home as nice as you can.

ACKNOWLEDGEMENTS

Thank you to Betty Borns, for her steadfast friendship and support through all the chapters of our lives. You are the best friend ever.

Thank you to Julie Seedorf, the Word Whippers Critique Group: William Anderson, Cathlene Buchholtz, Dale Butler, Barb Danson, and Mary Rodgers for their support and critiques of FATAL FLIP, A Home Renovator Mystery.

ABOUT THE AUTHOR

M. E. Bakos has published several short stories in national women's magazines. Her love of mysteries has led to writing cozies. Her first mystery short story, "Carpe Diem or Murder at the Carp Fest" appeared in the *Festival of Crime: a SINC Anthology*. Her second, "Perfect Storm . . . Perfect Murder" is published in *Dark Side of the Loon*, May, 2018, also a SINC Anthology.

She is an enthusiastic fan of home improvement shows and has done numerous home projects through the years. A fun fact: she interned with a Minneapolis non-profit housing agency, where she researched, wrote, and edited a monthly home improvement newsletter.

She is a member of Twin Cities Sisters in Crime, the SINC Guppies Group, and an alumna of the University of Minnesota. FATAL FLIP is her first home improvement cozy mystery novel.

She lives with her husband, Joe Sebesta, and their spoiled Morkie (Maltese/Yorkie), Chipper, in Minnesota.

If you enjoyed this book, please consider posting a review on your favorite retailer's website.

Next in Series:

DEADLY FLIP, A Home Renovator Mystery, #2
LETHAL FLIP, A Home Renovator Mystery, #3

Visit M. E. Bakos on Facebook

Or at: mebakos.wixsite.com/author

FATAL FLIP, DEADLY FLIP, and **LETHAL FLIP** received five-star reviews from Reader's Favorite.

www.ingramcontent.com/pod-product-compliance
Lightning Source LLC
Chambersburg PA
CBHW020337180726
47991CB00020B/1733